Jo Beall studied English Literature and Economic History in South Africa before completing a PhD at the London School of Economics. She taught international development at the LSE, was Deputy Vice Chancellor at the University of Cape Town and was Global Director of Education and Cultural Engagement at the British Council.

Meadowlands Dawn is Jo's debut novel, a work inspired by her own experience as an activist and political prisoner under Apartheid, in South Africa.

'A thoughtful, generous fiction about the ever-unfinished business of South Africa's past.'

Jonny Steinberg – author of Winnie & Nelson

'This exciting debut novel is an authentic take on the experience of detention in apartheid South Africa in the 1980s, describing the twists and turns of political deception, brutality and survival. Though this is in part a sombre read, it is shot through with ironic humour, with resilience and, finally, with hope for the healing of the central character and the flawed nation she represents. Meadowlands Dawn allows the reader to gain a fresh perspective on apartheid South Africa and its aftermath.'

Lindy Stiebel – Professor Emeritus University of KwaZulu-Natal

'What happens when you revisit your first love, and your first great loss? What happens when this loving and losing took place during the iconic, epic struggle for justice in Apartheid South Africa? What is true, what can be trusted? Who is what they seem? In this debut novel Jo Beall puts the aptly named Verity – a white South African young women in love – at the pounding heart of the struggle. There is no sugar-coating the raw, slimy, visceral nature of torture, interrogation, age, sex and death. But in a narrative where to be able to wash, and to wake up free, there is a search for the cleansing of a truth which could be lived with, which could reconcile the self, on all sides of the Apartheid struggle. In Meadowlands Dawn no one is a hero. Everyone their own partial warrior. And the quest for a reconciling truth that can release from the captivities of the past, is thrilling.'

Alison Phipps – Professor of Languages and Intercultural Studies and UNESCO Chair, University of Glasgow, author of Call and No Response: 30 Prayers in Genocidal Times (2024)

MEADOWLANDS DAWN

JO BEALL

époque press

Published by Epoque Press in 2024

Typeset in EB Garamond Regular, EB Garamond, Regular
Italic , EB Garamond, Bold Italic & PF Fuel.
Typesetting & cover design by Ten Storeys®

Printed and bound in Great Britain by
Clays Ltd, Elcograf S.p.A.

British Library Cataloguing-in-Publication Data
A catalogue record for this book is available from
the British Library

ISBN 978-1-7391-881-1-5 (paperback edition).

Author's Note

Meadowlands Dawn is a work of fiction, and all its characters exist only within these pages. Some of the things that happen are based on real events, which thankfully are now confined to history.

The terms black and African are used interchangeably in South Africa to refer to black South Africans indigenous to the continent. The term coloured is used in South African parlance to refer to people of mixed race, and both terms are used there. Indian South Africans descend either from Hindu indentured labourers who arrived in South Africa between 1860 and 1913, courtesy of the British, and Muslim traders who arrived during this same period. I sometimes refer to Indians and coloureds collectively as brown, or in Afrikaans, bruinmense. White South Africans descend mainly from the Dutch who arrived in the 17th century and who today speak Afrikaans, and English speakers who came in various waves of immigration from Great Britain during the 19th and 20th centuries.

Apartheid (1948 to 1994) refers to the laws and practices of racial segregation that were imposed by the all-white, mainly Afrikaans state, which required different racial groups to live in separate areas and use separate public facilities. It was in force from the time the Nationalist Party came into power in 1948 until the first non-racial democratic elections in 1994. The Prohibition of Mixed Marriages Act, Act No 55 of 1949, prohibited marriages between whites and non-whites and by definition, intimacy of any kind. It was the first piece of apartheid legislation to be passed and one of the first to be repealed in 1985, although social attitudes were slow to catch up with legislative change.

The Internal Security Act 74 of 1982 gave the apartheid

Government broad powers to restrict people, public gatherings and to serve banning orders, house arrest and detention of people without trial. Section 29 allowed for the warrantless arrest and indefinite detention of those suspected of terrorist offences for the purposes of interrogation. Detainees were held incommunicado and in solitary confinement and torture was common. The Act was progressively repealed between 1990 and 2005.

The post-apartheid period officially began with the first non-racial democratic elections held between the 26th and 29th April 1994, which were overseen by the Independent Electoral Commission (IEC), following a period of protracted and often fraught negotiations that lasted over four years. The African National Congress (ANC), whose slate included the Congress of South African Trade Unions (COSATU) and the South African Communist Party (SACP), won 62 per cent of the vote. They formed a Government of National Unity with the former ruling National Party (NP), and the Inkatha Freedom Party (IFP), both of which won more than 20 seats in the National Assembly, which as its first act, elected Nelson Mandela as President.

Since 1994 South Africa has had five presidents, all from the ruling ANC Party: Nelson Mandela, Thabo Mbeki, Kgalema Motlanthe, Jacob Zuma, and Cyril Ramaphosa. In 2024 the election results saw for the first time the ANC lose its absolute majority. Among the main opposition parties is the Democratic Alliance, a former white party with a stronghold in local and provincial government in the Western Cape Province, with whom the ANC is now ruling in a government of national unity (GNU). The leftist populist Economic Freedom Fighters (EFF) was formed in 2013 by Julius Malema, an expelled member of the ANC Youth League (ANCYL). Jacob Zuma, who was president between 2009 and 2018, and who was forced to step down due to corruption charges, continues to command support in Kwa-Zulu Natal (KZN) Province and backed a new party, uMkhonto we Sizwe (MK), named after the armed wing of the ANC, although Zuma himself was barred by the IEC from running in the May 2024 general election.

The following authors helped provide context on South African politics during the times in which the novel was set: *Unfinished Business, South Africa, Apartheid and Truth* by Terry Bell (2001); *Askari* by Jacob Dlamini (2014); *Red Road to Freedom, A History of the South African Communist Party 1921-2021* by Tom Lodge (2021); *Shades of Difference, Mac Maharaj and the Struggle for South Africa* by Padraig O'Malley (2007); *The ANC Spy Bible* by Moe Shaik (2020).

For Lily and Ted

Don't stare, it's rude
And empathy is rape.
And kindness is, like hunger, loss of self.

What is the right distance for touching?

They say if you want a dog to come to you
stand still, don't run towards it, calling.

And when it comes?

*From Aching by Karen Press, The Canary's Songbook,
first published by Carcanet UK in 2002.*

MEADOWLANDS
DAWN

PART 1

PART 1

The key hung from the warder's waist like a menacing prick. He felt for it, played with it in his hand and then twisted it in the lock. Verity followed him in, clutching the plastic shopper bulging with the items they had told her to pack. The warder cast a quick eye over the cell and inclined his immense neck to indicate to the two guards where they should put the metal bedframe. Scraping it through the heavy iron door, the guards dropped the frame in the corner and threw on a foam mattress, a pillow, a corporation blue sheet and a coarse grey blanket.

'Not quite what you're used to, hey,' said the warder.

'That bed only has three legs.'

'If you were black like these guys,' the warder said, nodding towards the guards, 'you'd just have a mat. Consider yourself lucky.'

'I'll take the mat,' Verity retorted with contrived bravado.

'I'll tell what you will do Juffrou Saunders, you'll shut up! We're busy people and you're not the only blerrie prisoner in here tonight. I've had enough of you fokking politicals, thinking you're something special.' He slammed the door behind him, leaving Verity standing alone under the glare of a single lightbulb.

Above the door through which they had entered was a thin mesh-covered strip of window. In the wall opposite was another locked iron door. The bed had been placed against one side wall and protruding from the other was a built-in wedge of concrete. Verity sat down on it and all the fear she might have reasonably felt over the last twenty-four hours took full possession of her. Eyes darting, she located a toilet in the corner concealed on one side by a low concrete wall. She pulled off her joggers and knickers and straddled the bowl, trying to avoid touching the brown-stained porcelain. She reached out to steady herself, and her hand scraped against something crusty on the wall. It was row upon row of four lines crossed out by a fifth, where a previous occupant must have counted down the days of their incarceration in their own excrement. Verity snapped back her hand and looked around for toilet paper. There was none. Fighting waves of nausea, she looked for a wash hand basin, but could not see one. No sink. No tap. No bucket. No water.

She crawled over to her bag, pulled out the pack of travel tissues she had packed and tried to clean herself as best she could. Pulling her knickers and joggers back on she dropped the soiled tissue into the toilet, flushed and watched as the slow run of brown water swirled it away. She slumped down on the bed. It tilted and the blanket slid to the floor. It was too hot for it anyway. Sliding under the sheet, she wriggled along the bedframe to balance herself and lay there rigid, longing for the kind of sleep that allowed escape from thinking. She checked her wrist for the time, but they had taken her watch. When next she heard the clang of the cell door, she was prostrate on the floor beneath the bed suffused by the hollow feeling that accompanies exhaustion and fear.

The morning warder was a homely looking woman in her fifties. She entered the cell unannounced followed by two black boys not yet in double figures, far too young to be in an adult prison. One carried a tin tray with an enamel dish and mug on it, the other a toilet roll and a slice of red carbolic soap.

'Your breakfast,' said the warder as she handed Verity a box of sanitary towels, 'and these are for your monthlies. Sometimes the flush on the toilet isn't great so you might need to push them through if they get stuck.'

'Can I have some cleaning materials? The wall by the toilet is filthy.'

'No, my dear, you can't. You'll manage.' The warder looked at her with a cold smile. 'I'm sure your comrades will have prepared you well for your stay here. You'll settle in in no time at all.'

'And where do I go to wash?'

'You don't go anywhere. You're in solitary. That's why you've got a courtyard.'

One of the boys took a bunch of keys from the warder and moved to the back wall of the cell where he unlocked the other iron door. It took both the boys to push it wide open and fix it permanently open on its hook. An insipid light filtered through the frame.

'This is where you wash,' said the warder as she strode out into the courtyard with Verity following behind her. 'There's a shower there.' The warder pointed to a pipe in the wall, below which was a lever. 'You push this up and water comes. You need to be quick. Not too sure how long the water runs for. Right now, you should eat your breakfast. You'll be needing your energy.'

The warder looked Verity up and down, turned on her heel

and walked back through the cell. When she heard the cell door slam shut Verity slid down the courtyard wall, clutching the box of sanitary towels. Nearby she heard the squeak of the wheels of the breakfast trolley and more faintly, the far-off voices of other prisoners as they called to each other in isiZulu. Determined to stay focused, she began to run through the movement's commandments for comrades in prison.

Commandment One: comrades should find ways to keep track of time. She had been arrested yesterday, Wednesday, the 26th of October, so today was Thursday, and it was morning.

Commandment Two: comrades should keep up their strength. She willed herself to her feet, went back into the cell and examined the tin tray on the concrete wedge. Lifting the greaseproof paper from the enamel dish she revealed mealie meal porridge, topped with a thick crust of sugar. Her stomach clenched and she let the paper fall. There was a tin mug from which the handle had been removed. She cupped it, trying to ignore the phosphorescent swirl of grease on its surface. She took a sip of the tepid grey liquid, which she supposed was tea. It was very sweet. She stuck her finger in the mielie pap and licked it. It was without salt but bearable if she didn't think about the texture. She picked up the balsawood spoon and forced down a couple of mouthfuls.

Commandment Three: comrades should keep themselves clean. Verity lifted her arm. She could smell her own body odour. She stripped off her joggers, T-shirt, and underwear, tossed them on the wedge and crossed the courtyard to the shower. She examined her slice of carbolic soap. The brand name was Lifebuoy, an irony not lost on her. Standing under the pipe she pushed up the lever and it delivered a weak flow of cold water. She soaped herself up, shivering as much from the sense of exposure as from the temperature. She closed her eyes and tried to savour the sensation of the water on her skin when the sound of metal on metal made her turn. Over her shoulder she saw a uniformed officer standing by an iron gate in the courtyard, leading from what she presumed must be another outside corridor. She had missed this third door and its gate on her cursory look around. Verity crossed her arms over her breasts and shouted at him to get out. He took a step closer, and she backed up against the rough courtyard wall.

'No need to be shy Juffrou Saunders. Come on, give me another look at those tits. Not sure they're enough for me but you might be lucky,' he said as he lifted his baton over his crotch and made a thrusting motion.

Verity stared at him, pressing herself harder against the courtyard wall, wondering if anyone would hear her if she screamed.

'Maybe another time,' the warder sneered and spat on the floor before turning on his heel and locking the courtyard gate behind him.

Verity slumped to the floor, wrapped her arms tightly about her knees, pulling them in close to her chest, and lapsed into a state of near numbness.

2

A cone of torchlight washed the walls yellow and a man's voice ordered Verity to get up and follow him from the cell. This is it, she thought, bracing herself.

Tapping his baton against his open palm, the same officer who had intruded on her shower led her along a series of dismal corridors. As they walked she went over Commandment Four in her mind: comrades should prepare themselves for interrogation. The rule was to hold out for three days, if possible. If comrades broke under questioning after that it was unfortunate but forgivable. Three days gave anyone you might incriminate time to put their house in order, like getting out of the country. It was only day two. She had to stay strong, although she hoped that by now Tariq and Imran would be safely in Swaziland.

They reached an elevator and ascended in silence. The officer with the baton stood uncomfortably close behind her. His breath was hot against the back of her neck and smelt of cheap brandy. She tried to stay focused, to keep her thoughts collected, and so, turned to Commandment Five: comrades should rehearse their legend. She was confident she knew it, she had rehearsed it often enough. The purpose of the legend was to confuse the security police, to make them believe that she was driving Tariq and Imran to the Swaziland border, although in truth they would have already left the country by other means. When they found her at the border alone, she was to tell them she was visiting a friend who taught at the international school in Mbabane. That is exactly what happened, so she was confident the legend had worked. All she had to do now was to stick to it.

At the seventh floor they exited the elevator and the officer shoved her into a small, sparsely furnished room. Alone, she circled the space, pacing the stained tiled floor under the harsh glare of a fluorescent ceiling tube. As her heartbeat returned to a recognisable rhythm she stopped to read a notice pinned on the back of an internal door. They were instructions on what to do in the event of a fire, written in English and Afrikaans, but not isiZulu. Perhaps they assumed black people couldn't read, Verity thought in disgust, either that or they didn't care if black people went up in flames with the building. As she read the sign the door opened and a man in jeans and a white short-sleeved shirt summoned her into an adjoining room.

Standing in front of a desk in the centre of the room was an older man, tall but of the flimsiest construction, his trim moustache and neatly combed hair almost effete. As Verity entered he regarded her over the top of steepled fingers, and she noticed his nails were neatly clipped and manicured.

'This is Major Anton Viljoen, Head of National Intelligence. He came down from Pretoria by helicopter, especially to attend your case,' said the younger man as he sat down on a swivel chair at the desk and opened a file.

The Major picked up a sheet of paper from the file and read it, holding it close to his face. Verity wondered why such a senior person had flown to Durban to speak to her in person. Surely, it was Imran and Tariq they were interested in. She didn't warrant the attention of the big guys.

'Juffrou Saunders, I assume you know why you're here?' he said, looking up from the form, his question measured and controlled.

'Because you represent a racist state that ignores people's human rights.' Verity had prepared her script and was determined not to deviate from it.

'You are to be held indefinitely under Section 29 of the Internal Security Act,' said Viljoen, spelling out what Verity knew to be the worst of all possible outcomes.

Section 29 meant solitary confinement, no trial, no visitors, no letters, no parcels, no time piece, no reading matter, no recourse to lawyers, no charges brought, and no end in sight. He returned the paper to the desk and left the room, and in that moment Verity realised that in Major Anton Viljoen she had confronted not censure but resolute indifference.

In the pause that followed the only sound to be heard was the younger man's pen as it scratched its way across his ledger. With a knock at the door he stopped writing, put down his pen and shouted, 'kom.'

'Meneer! Goeie môre Kaptein.' The uniformed officer who had escorted her from her cell stood to attention in front of the desk and saluted.

'Get on with it,' the captain ordered, handing him the paper left behind by Major Viljoen.

'Juffrou Verity Margaret Saunders,' the officer read. 'We have reason to believe you have been furthering the aims of the

A.N.C.' He spat out the acronym in Afrikaans. At the best of times it was a no-nonsense language, but in his mouth it sounded like verbal abuse.

'Are you charging me?'

'We is informing you. Furthering the aims of a banned organisation is a serious crime.' He looked to his senior for approval, but the captain's attention was with his ledger.

'What you do is a crime,' Verity said more calmly than she felt. 'You put people in prison without charge. That's a crime. You shoot people in the back when they run from your guns. That's a crime. And you're breaking international law by detaining me without charge or trial.'

'Be that as it may, you is the one who is detained, Juffrou Saunders. Now tell me who trained you to use an AK47?'

'Don't be ridiculous.'

'We don't tolerate cheek Juffrou. When did you went for military training?'

'Let me think. Perhaps I fitted it in between going to work and my supermarket shop.'

There was a suppressed snort from behind the desk and Verity looked over to the captain, who had picked up his pen again and was quietly making notes. He was good looking in a rugged way, she thought, his aquiline features at odds with his large rugby player's physique. His short sleeves exposed strong, tanned forearms and his thighs strained against the seams of his denims. His type was well-known to her, a grown version of the rougher boys who hung around the bus stop after school. His accent suggested he spoke English at home, although he appeared more than comfortable in the hybrid Afrikaans spoken in the police force and most government offices in Durban.

'Look at me Juffrou,' said the uniformed officer, jabbing a finger in his chest. 'I is the one representing the authorities right now.'

Verity wanted to laugh. He was jealous of the passing attention she had paid to his superior.

'Now stand up straight and tell me, where did you went for military training, the USSR or GDR?'

'You people have been trailing me around Durban for months. I think you'd know if I'd taken a trip abroad.'

'Don't get fokking smart with me.' He took a step forward and loomed over her, his brandy breath scoring the air.

Verity faltered as she tried to step back from the broken veins across his nose. 'Are you trying to frighten me, Sergeant?'

'Not at all, Verity.' This was the captain. 'Just give us something to go on and we can let you go. We're simply trying to establish how deep in you are. We're as keen as you to get this thing wrapped up.'

'I have not received military training in the Soviet Union or anywhere else,' Verity said decisively.

'What about at home with Tariq Randeree?' said the captain as he leant back in his chair and looked at her through amused blue-grey eyes. Then, with a flick of his head, he motioned for the officer to leave them.

'I have nothing to hide. My home is my home,' said Verity as the uniformed officer reluctantly left the room.

'We know a lot more about you than you think, Verity, although you're very good at giving us the slip, I'll give you that.'

'I've never done military training,' she said, holding his gaze but fighting a clutch of panic. 'And I'm a pacifist.'

'Ja, we know that. We've listened in on your arguments with Tariq over the rights and wrongs of the armed struggle.'

Verity allowed the silence between them to widen, wondering when and how they'd done that.

'How would you define yourself Verity, in terms of your politics, I mean?'

'I'm an anti-apartheid activist,' she said after a pause, 'a very committed one.'

'Interesting. You see, we think you're a criminal, maybe even a terrorist.' So, don't you think it's time you told us exactly why you were stopped at the roadblock before you reached the Swazi border?'

'I was visiting a friend who teaches at the international school in Mbabane,' Verity replied.

She thought back to the incident. The police who had searched her car had been thorough. They had looked in the glove compartment, beneath the seats, the trunk, under the bonnet, taking their time. They had opened her overnight bag and tossed her clothes across the back seat, pinging a pair of floral knickers at her like a catapult. They had even gone through the Tupperware with her uneaten food from the journey, un-scrunching the waxed paper and checking it for notes. They had taken their time and were unfazed as the sound of car horns had grown more insistent from the traffic building up behind them. When they finished their search they had told Verity that her little adventure was over and that she should go home. That was all. So yes, the legend had worked.

'What time were you stopped?'

'Around eleven a.m.'

'You must have had to get up very early to reach the Swazi border from Durban by then.'

'I did.'

'If you say so.' The captain checked his wrist. 'I think we're done for now, Verity. We'll speak again soon,' he said as he rose from his chair and pressed a bell on the desk.

When they got back to her cell the uniformed officer pushed her in and stood at the door tapping his baton against the frame.

'You is going to pay for cheeking me, Juffrou Saunders. Perhaps I'll be back for your next shower.' He grabbed Verity's arm and twisted it.

As her ragged breath stained the air, Verity felt the same sense of awful inevitability that had washed over her the night she was arrested.

*   *   *

Imran had warned Verity that agreeing to be decoy meant arrest was, if not inevitable, then highly likely, and she had been disbelieving when Tariq concurred. Sitting absolutely still and upright, his splendid profile perfectly poised, he had met her eye with a cool and steady gaze. Imran had placed his hands down on the table, hands that looked like they had never seen a day's labour, despite all the detonators he had boasted about wiring. Slowly he nodded his head. A dread settled in Verity's gut.

When she arrived back in Durban, after her return drive from the Swazi border, Verity found a plastic Pick-n-Pay carrier bag and began filling it with what she might need in prison: a change of clothes, a couple of sets of underwear, and a towel. She had located the pink satin sponge bag her mother had given her for her birthday - what had she been thinking, it was so not her? In it she put her toothbrush, toothpaste, a facecloth and deodorant, then looked around wondering what else she might need. She added nail clippers, a brush, a travel pack of tissues and the remains of a packet of paracetamol.

From her bedside drawer she extracted a tampon and made a small incision in the paper cover, sliding out the plug from the tube and replacing it with a thin furl of paper. She tucked the tampon at the bottom of the sponge bag and put in another on top of it. Next, she left a note for Louise, her long-suffering sister. She put it in the freezer under some lamb chops. The security police would never think to look for anything there, Verity thought, and Lou being Lou, she was bound to defrost and clean out the fridge if she and Tariq were gone for any length of time. Then she made herself a mug of tea and lay back on the sofa to wait.

When they came for her Verity had watched as they searched cupboards and drawers, shelves and desks, making a mental inventory of what they took; mainly Tariq's books. When they were done, they told her to pack a track suit and jumper, signalling she might be inside for a long time. A firm hand on her shoulder then steered her down the stairs to a waiting police car. Verity felt numb although her body had left clues as to her mental state, traces of sweat lining the underarms of her shirt. Doors had cracked open to reveal the inquisitive eyes of neighbours. It was not the first time that the illegal inter-racial couple upstairs had given them cause for intrigue and complaint.

Verity abandoned all effort at sleep on the three-legged bed. She dragged the mattress onto the floor, propped the frame against the wall and lay down to go over the interrogation in her head. She gave herself eight out of ten for focus and hoped that by now Tariq and Imran would be safely away. When sleep eventually came it was fitful and she was woken early by the dawn light creeping in from the courtyard door.

'Missed seeing your tits last night, Juffrou. Hurry up, don't waste my time, asseblief,' said the uniformed officer as he threw open the cell door.

Verity tried to resist his grip on her arm, but he tightened it further, pulling and pushing her as they made their way along the prison corridors. She had no idea what time it was, but she was still drowsy and very hungry. As she stumbled along beside the officer she felt the walls closing in around her. She scrutinised the chips in the concrete floor in order to regain her composure and noticed a long streak of brown that looked very much like dried blood. Her heart pummelled her ribs and sucked the breath from her lungs.

The captain sat waiting for her in the interrogation room, but this time Viljoen was nowhere to be seen. Verity decided that his brief appearance had been designed to put the frighteners on her and to show her the state was taking her case seriously.

'So, Verity, it's time to tell me more about your bungled trip to Swaziland.' The captain pushed a hand through his thick brown hair. 'So we don't waste time, I should make you aware that we know you checked into the Holiday Inn in Ermelo along with Tariq Randeree and Imran Malik the night before you were stopped at the roadblock.' The captain pressed the bell on the desk and a skinny young officer with a bad case of acne entered carrying a reel-to-reel tape recorder. He placed it on the desk and began threading the tape, looping it around the reels. The captain sat with his arms folded, regarding Verity impassively. Once he had finished with the tape the young officer compressed the play button and Imran Malik's voice filled the room.

'To secure our escape we will cross the border using a secret route known only to a few of us.' Imran cleared his throat. 'We need someone to act as decoy.'

'What does that mean?' Verity heard herself ask.

'Decoys are designed to be caught, in order to let others escape,' Imran replied.

'That's you, Verity,' came Tariq's disembodied voice.

'The consequences will be lighter for you because you are...' Imran paused, 'well, white. Anyway, if we want a non-racial future in this country, we need some whiteys to take one for the team.' She hadn't noticed Imran's cynical chuckle at the time.

'The work of our cell has been compromised.' Tariq's voice came in, rendered somewhat tinny by the tape. 'Ever since my detention, surveillance on us has increased. We're stymied. The leadership has ordered Imran and I to leave the country. We will travel together in one car and you will follow separately behind. We will spend the night at the Holiday Inn at Ermelo.'

'Are we all able to stay there?' she heard herself ask.

'Yes,' said Imran. 'It's an international hotel so it accepts guests of colour, though usually not darker than brown.' He chuckled again. 'At dawn, our contact will pick us up and take us to a secret crossing place used by the ANC. Later that morning you will drive to the official South African border post and enter Swaziland. They will think you are taking us, so will be looking out for your car. This will give us the cover we need.'

The captain signalled for the tape machine to be turned off, and a heavy silence filled the room. Verity looked at him and felt herself colour. 'You knew why I was at the border all along,' she said. 'Did those SAP guys really expect to find Imran and Tariq with me?'

'Of course not,' he grinned. 'As you've just heard, we knew you'd been set up as a decoy. Those guys used you so they could skip the country, Verity, then left you to face the music. What was your boyfriend Tariq thinking?'

'I don't know what goes on in Tariq's head.'

'Probably safer that way,' the captain said with a grim laugh. He dismissed the young officer and waited until the door closed behind him before continuing. 'Your room was in a different wing of the hotel, Verity. Did you see the guys again after you got there?'

'Just Tariq, briefly,' she conceded, 'in my room.'

'What did you talk about?'

'Nothing, we just said goodbye.' Verity was confident that anything they had said could not have been overheard. They had turned on all the taps in the bathroom, pulled the string of the extractor fan, and ran the shower. It was a familiar drill. She and Tariq had stood naked under the water, holding each other, listening to the rise and fall of the other's breathing. He had told her he was leaving earlier than planned, his whispers coming at her from places she barely recognised. It was as if another version of him was inhabiting his familiar exterior. She tried to arouse him, but he had removed her hand.

'Don't,' he'd whispered, 'if I didn't manage it tonight, I couldn't bear it. Promise me you'll look after my boy.'

'She might be a girl.'

'Well, if she's anything like her mother, she'll be a little warrior.' In that moment a lost tenderness returned to his voice.

They had dressed in silence. Tariq went over to the tray he had ordered for her from room service and lifted the dome. He pointed to a piece of paper tucked under the plate. She nodded, watched him take two swift bites of the hamburger, stuff a handful of chips in his mouth and head for the door. She followed him, skimming a trail of ketchup off his chin. He put her finger to his lips, licked off the ketchup and closed the door quietly behind him.

'Whenever you're ready, Verity.' The captain's voice summoned her back to the interrogation room.

'I don't know what more I can tell you. We said goodbye, Tariq ate a hamburger from room service, then he left. That's it.' Involuntarily, her hands moved to the thickening around her waist.

'Room service?'

'Yes, Tariq had food sent up for me, but I wasn't hungry.'

'Was that wise? Surely, he must have known that it could have connected the two of you and put you at risk.'

'I was already at risk don't you think, given I was the sodding decoy?'

'You've got spirit, Verity, I have to admit. I suspect you shared more than a hamburger. But I'm not interested in what you did. I want to know what Tariq said.'

'He said it was too dangerous to wait until dawn, so they were leaving earlier than originally planned.'

'Did you believe him?'

'Yes, and I saw them leave. It was around one in the morning. I heard an engine, so I went and looked out of the window.'

'What kind of car was it?'

'I couldn't tell.' It was a Nissan Micra, but she wasn't going to give him that.

'Colour?'

'White.' No great give away. White cars were ubiquitous in a country doing permanent battle with the heat.

'Did you get the registration number?'

Verity shook her head.

'And you're sure Tariq and Imran were together?'

'It was dark, but I saw Tariq getting into the back. Imran must have been in the driver's seat.'

'As far as I am aware, Verity, Imran doesn't drive.'

'Oh…that's right. Maybe he was in the passenger seat. I don't know. Why do you care where Imran was sitting?'

'We care because when Imran reached the safe house in Swaziland, Tariq was not with him.' He paused, allowing the news to sink in. 'Where is Tariq, Verity?'

'I don't know,' she said, as waves of nausea beat through her. 'I definitely saw him get in the back of the car.'

That was all she knew for certain. Alone in her hotel room she had mentally followed his journey, imagining him crawling through a slash in a barbed wire fence and scrambling to safety on Swazi soil. The last glimpse in her mind's eye had been of a moon-bleached ghoul scrambling up from the red earth and running across a vast expanse of veld.

4

Back in her cell, Verity sat on the concrete ledge wondering what had happened to Tariq. She had definitely seen him get in the car and she had seen it leave. How could Imran have made it without him? If he was at the safe house alone, where on earth was Tariq now? Perhaps the captain was lying to her, she thought, trying to confuse her, wanting to trip her up or get her to say something that would incriminate her further. She opened her plastic carrier bag, with the things they had allowed her to bring, and rummaged through the pink satin sponge bag for the tampon she had packed, the one into which she had secreted the slip of paper which Tariq had left for her on the tray in her room at the Holiday Inn in Ermelo. She couldn't bring herself to read it at the time but now wondered if it could hold a clue as to his whereabouts. She was about to open the tube when she heard the sound of a key turn in her cell door. She quickly dropped the tampon back into the sponge bag and kicked the plastic carrier aside.

One of the young black boys entered carrying a lunch tray. He placed the tray next to her on the concrete wedge and shyly gave Verity the salute of the ANC, his elbow bent into his waist, his hand slightly raised and clenched into a fist.

'Thank you,' said Verity, warily. She looked at the tray and asked, 'what treats do we have today?'

'Same, same,' the boy replied, lowering his arm and backing out of the cell.

He was right, the food was the same for every meal on every day. Mealie meal porridge for breakfast with a crust of sugar on top, for supper the same porridge came with watery cabbage and for lunch, as now, the pap was served with beetroot and limp lettuce. Verity sat cross-legged on the floor and balanced the tray on the mattress. She was supposed to be eating for two, so she had to do her best to digest it all. As a way of masking the taste she imagined she was sitting around the Karim's table, eating one of Ma's famous curries.

*   *   *

The home of Aziz and Ma Karim was cramped and noisy, but the aromas of Ma's cooking wafted a welcome through their always open door. Ma was Tariq's aunt and as different from her widowed sister, Fatima Randeree, as any woman could be. The Karim family had welcomed Verity into their lives without question, simply because Tariq had chosen her, and because she was a friend of their daughter Yasmin, Tariq's cousin.

The weekend after Tariq was released from jail Ma Karim had made all his favourites; chicken pasanda, lamb curry, mint and coriander chutney, and piles of rumali roti. That night he had shared his guest of honour status with Imran Malik, who was made welcome and admired by the family for having spent ten years on Robben Island with other veterans of the struggle.

Tariq had eaten hungrily, scraping his plate clean with one and then another freshly cooked roti and the younger children of the family stared at him with unapologetic curiosity, dawdling whimsically over their own plates of food.

'You see, they starved him!' one of them remarked, causing Tariq to pause and try to match Imran's deliberate pace.

'Why do you eat so slowly Imran? You were also in jail,' asked another.

'After ten years I tend to keep the habits I developed on the Island. One of them is eating my food slowly. We did it in part to make our meals last, but we also made sure we always kept some food back so everyone had something. You see, the warders would often punish comrades by denying them food so we would share with that prisoner what little we had saved so he didn't have to go to sleep on an empty stomach.'

'Did they give you a bed? What about a toilet? What did you eat?' Young heads turned from Tariq to Imran, questions flying in different directions.

'The food was edible but nothing like Ma's,' said Tariq, wiping his mouth with a paper serviette. 'Apologies for devouring it so quickly.'

'Are you heroes like Nelson Mandela and Yusuf Dadoo?' One boy asked.

'No,' Imran protested, 'but I'm pleased to hear that you know about our struggle's leaders.'

'Give Tariq and Imran some space you kids,' said Aziz. 'Wash your hands and go and watch TV. Let the adults have a chance to talk.'

Throughout the meal Mrs Randeree had kept a protective hand on Tariq's arm, looking at Imran with unabashed awe, whilst shooting Verity dirty looks from time to time, letting her know she didn't welcome her presence at the table. Verity had given up trying to ingratiate herself with Tariq's mother, who had set her heart on brokering an arranged marriage with a nice Muslim girl worthy of her only son, the first in the family to go to university, and a doctor.

*   *   *

Remembering the flavours and warmth of that meal transformed the bleakness of her lunch, but as she bent down to put the tray on the floor by the cell door, Verity felt a twinge in her back. Commandment Six: comrades should adopt an exercise routine, even if in confined spaces. Even though she ached with exhaustion she knew she had to keep active, so she went out into the courtyard and began to circle it. Three short steps down one side, then three along the next, and the next and the next. As she walked around in square circles she heard the black prisoners calling to each other and then a tenor began to sing. The song was *Shoshaloza*, a song about migrant workers heading by train to work in the mines. She picked up her pace as more voices joined in. They ended their medley by singing Nkosi Sikel' iAfrika. Verity tried to sing along in a voice strangled by emotion, remembering the first time she had heard the anthem of the ANC at the funeral of Agatha Khumalo. It had been her first time in a black township and when her feelings for Tariq had stirred.

*   *   *

The funeral was not long after Verity's chance meeting with Tariq in the stationery store at the medical school where she worked as a secretary. She had been surprised to find a doctor struggling with the old Gestetner, smudges of ink staining his starched white coat. Duplicating lecture notes and exam papers was a secretary's job, well hers at least. She hated the business of pinning the waxed stencils on the drum, then waiting, with stinging eyes in air heavy with the smell of spirit, for the last sheet of blurry violet type to flop into the tray.

The doctor had whipped up his printed sheets and left, his stethoscope lashing the door as he pulled it behind him. The waxed template was still on the drum. Curious, Verity gave the handle another turn. The single sheet she printed off was neither lecture notes nor exam questions, but a pamphlet announcing a funeral:

WE THE PEOPLE OF SOUTH AFRICA, BLACK, BROWN AND WHITE, HOLD THE FUTURE OF THIS COUNTRY IN OUR HANDS. COMRADE AGATHA KHUMALO NEVER SHIRKED FROM HER DUTY AND NOR MUST WE. POWER MUST BE EXTRACTED FROM THE GRIP OF OUR APARTHEID OPPRESSORS. THEIR RULE IS UNJUST AND ILLEGITIMATE. SOUTH AFRICANS OF EVERY HUE MUST STAND TOGETHER TO RECLAIM WHAT THEY HAVE STOLEN FOR OURSELVES AND FUTURE GENERATIONS.

The door was thrown open. In its frame was the silhouette of a stiff white coat.

'I think you have something of mine.' The doctor's tone was terse.

Verity handed him the page.

'Who are you? I haven't seen you around,' he said.

'I'm the new secretary in Obs and Gynae. I work for

Professor Sithole.'

'I trust I can rely on your discretion?' Creases formed across his high forehead.

'Of course!' She smiled brightly, conscious of herself.

'I'm serious,' he said.

'So am I. Who is Agatha Khumalo?'

'She was a nurse at this hospital, a brave woman who fought for the rights of health workers. She stood up for the porters, the cleaners, people we step over while they're on their knees cleaning our floors, and here I include black doctors.'

'And white secretaries,' she said, feeling herself coquettish.

A shadow of humour crossed his face and then was gone. He retrieved the stencil and Verity fetched an envelope from the cupboard, holding open its mouth to take the inky master copy. As he leaned over she caught a whiff of Imperial Leather soap on his skin. He straightened quickly, as if to muffle any suggestion of intimacy.

'Do you want me to take this? I dispose of exam stencils very securely.'

'This is a little different, wouldn't you say?' There was a snap to his voice.

'I guess. Can I come to the funeral?'

'There won't be many whites there.'

'It says on your pamphlet you want people of every hue. I can be the blue one.' She pointed jokily at her blouse.

As he took it in, its colour, her shape, the top button straining against her breasts, Verity felt his regard like idle fingertips.

'How old are you?' he asked, shifting his gaze.

'Old enough. I have the key to the door.' Thrilled at her own daring, she couldn't believe she was flirting with a doctor, an Indian doctor at that.

'I'll see if I can find someone to give you a lift. What's your name by the way?'

'Verity Saunders.'

'Randeree,' he said, holding out his hand. 'Tariq Randeree. Anaesthetics.'

Tariq's cousin, Yasmin Karim, was also a doctor, specialising in public health. She was quiet as they drove to Kwa Mashu and Verity stopped trying to initiate conversation. As they entered the township they passed a corrugated shambles of shacks, which gave way to rows and rows of identical matchbox houses. Yasmin parked near the market and told Verity to remember where the car was in case they got separated. If this happened, which was likely, she said Verity should place herself among older women and return to the car as soon as the proceedings were over.

Carried along by the crowds, Verity followed the mourners down the dusty street into the stadium. She found a group of elderly women who budged up to make space for her.

'Stay with me, sister,' said a grandmotherly woman in the uniform of a church choir. 'I'll make sure you stay safe.'

Massed voices sang *Hamba Kahle* as they handed Agatha Khumalo into the safekeeping of her ancestors.

'You know what they are saying?' the woman asked.

'I know hamba kahle means goodbye, literally go carefully, I think, but I don't know the one they are singing now.'

'*Senzeni Na?* They are asking, what have we done that you are doing this to us?'

A group of younger activists took over the singing next. They began to dance, stamping their feet, flattening the dry grass so that clouds of dust billowed beneath their tempo.

'We call this dance *toyi-toyi*,' said the woman, pulling a handkerchief from between her breasts and mopping her brow.

Umshini wami mshini wami, they now sang, beads of sweat flying from their pumped young bodies.

'What does this one mean?' Verity asked, sensing the mood shift.

'Eish, these young lions.' The elderly women were all shaking their heads.

'What are they saying?' Verity persisted.

'Bring me my machine gun,' the woman said, her eyes cast downwards.

She took a couple of damp cloths from her bag and handed one to Verity. 'I think they could make trouble for us. Put this over your face if they come with the teargas.'

All eyes were now on the rows of armed and agitated police, ranged at the edge of the crowd. Verity felt a tightening in her throat, and wondered if she should be scared. At that moment Tariq mounted the platform. He did so swiftly in a single leap, his slight stature emphasised by its juxtaposition next to the master of ceremonies, a large black man who Verity later came to know as Simeon Sikhakhane. Verity thought Tariq looked splendid in his collarless white shirt, the neck and cuffs finished with fine embroidery in a light gold coloured thread. As he raised his hands they glinted in the sunlight. He tapped the microphone, asked for silence, and quietly observed the crowd. The singing faded and the toyi-toyi drew to a staccato finish.

'Good afternoon comrades. My name is Tariq Randeree. I worked with Agatha Khumalo. Today we commend our comrade to her ancestors and her God. Comrades, I understand your frustration but soon victory will be ours. We must be patient but not too patient; vigilant but not inactive.' Tariq spoke in tones that simultaneously commanded and soothed. Sometimes his voice became so low that the crowd leaned forward in hushed silence to hear him.

'We are here to honour Agatha Khumalo for her contribution to our struggle and to remind ourselves of our own commitment, and so we will sing the movement's anthem, *Nkosi Sikelel' iAfrika*. The Apartheid state tries to forbid us from singing this because they are afraid of us, afraid of our numbers. Yet I ask you comrades, and I ask them too, how can we be punished for singing a hymn that asks for blessings on this beautiful land which we share?'

His authority, the reasonableness and the certitude of his words thrilled Verity. Wide-eyed with the newness of it all, her gaze never left him. She willed him to look her way, feeling sure she would be easy to pick out in the crowd as one of only a handful of whites, but he never did. His focus was on the restless young lions and the cordon of police, edgy on the periphery of the crowd. He raised his fist in the salute of the movement.

'Amandla!' he cried.

'Awethu!' they called back in resounding response. Power is ours.

The lined forces of the state maintained a steady presence but did not move. Protected by the religious dimensions of the funeral, the women warmed up to sing, their high carolling notes fusing with the bass voices of the men, arching in terrific unity. Verity didn't yet know the words, but the hairs on her arms and neck stood up in fevered salute.

5

'I see you didn't bother with a bra today. Nice to see you all excited for me,' said the uniformed officer as he stood in the doorway between the cell and the courtyard.

Verity, who had been watching the clouds change shape through the concrete beams that spanned the yard, stood frozen.

'Ja, man, you're in luck. They want to see you again. How's that, twice in one day? So, Juffrou, you'd better get moving and let me see those tits of yours bounce.'

Verity followed him as they traced the usual route along the warren of corridors to the elevator. As the door closed behind them the officer pushed her up against the side and grabbed hold of her breast.

'Hmm, you feeling good Juffrou, teasing me walking round with no bra? I think you're going to like it with me.'

'Get off me,' Verity growled and pushed at him, but he had her pinned.

'I know what you like,' he said, tightly twisting her nipple.

The ping of the elevator announced their arrival at the seventh floor, and as the door opened, he stepped back from her, whistling as he led her to the interrogation room. The door was open, but the room was empty. This time another chair had been set up to face the desk.

'You'll have to wait a little longer for a real taste of me,' said the officer as he pushed Verity into the room and closed the door.

Verity stood alone and waited. The last of the day's sun beat through the window and she noticed the ledge was covered in dust and dead flies. Shadows from the vertical blinds cast stripes across the floor and the desk. She wondered about trying to catch a glimpse of the outside world, but the internal door opened and the captain entered, followed by the young man with acne holding the tape machine under his arm.

'Sit down Verity, we have something we want you to hear.'

The young man set the machine down and Verity lowered herself onto the chair. He pressed down on the play button, and the reels began to turn. The room echoed with the unmistakeable British accent of Mavis Saunders.

'You are basically a good girl, Verity.'

How long had it been since she had heard the voice of her mother?

'You just have to give up this political nonsense. What I can't understand is why you don't choose someone more appropriate and give yourself the chance of having a proper relationship.'

'You mean someone white?'

Verity was taken aback by the sound of her own voice. Why is it you never sound the way you imagine yourself to, she thought.

'I know you think I'm prejudiced because Tariq's Indian, and I can't pretend I like it. Living together as you do is illegal. But that's not it. I've seen the two of you together. You hang on his every word as if he's some kind of oracle, and it doesn't become you. Anyway, why can't he find someone his own age?'

'You're not going to change my mind.'

A clearing sound in the back of her mother's throat, the click of a cigarette lighter, the intake of breath as she inhaled.

'Stirring things up like this, you've landed the country in a right mess,' her mother went on.

'The state of emergency is not just down to me, Mum.'

'I'm not saying you personally, but Tariq and his lot, agitating the blacks with their communist propaganda.'

'That's crap. Blacks don't need whites and Indians to tell them that their lives are shit.'

'No need for foul language, Verity. You've brought shame on your late father's memory.'

'Just hear me out Mum. I'm trying to be helpful. This organisation, it's called the Friends and Families of Detainees Committee, they can advise you, they...'

'I'm not getting involved with this committee or any other shady organisation associated with terrorists. If you end up in jail, be it on your own head.'

'Activists Mum, we're not terrorists, we're activists.'

'Call yourselves what you like Verity, you're playing with fire. Those so-called comrades of yours are just using you. They saw a gullible white face and took advantage of your good heart, and that includes Tariq. He groomed you. Daddy would be horrified.'

The reel flapped as the tape came to an end. Verity sat with her hands in her lap, picking at a broken nail. She remembered watching her late father's delicate fingers as he put in place the tiny pieces of the model ships he built, carefully rigging the miniature raking masts like the gentle man that he was. He had beautiful hands.

'You should have listened to your mother, Verity,' said the captain, breaking into her thoughts. 'She was right about Tariq. If you don't believe me, we have something else that might help you to have a rethink.'

The young officer changed the tape reel and when he pressed play it was Verity's voice which filled the room.

'Tariq, I've had enough. Imran is here yet again. He's sitting at the kitchen table doing the crossword. Does the man never sleep? I went to get some iced water and I was stark naked, and he just sat there leering at me.'

'I'm sorry, but we think his place is under surveillance and it's not safe for him there.'

'But it's okay for him to be here, making it unsafe for us?'

'They don't know he's here and I'm sorry, I should have warned you so you could have put on a robe.'

'Why should I have to wear a robe in my own home, Tariq? And why does he never bloody well go to bed?'

'He's slept odd hours ever since being on the Island. Ten year's is a long time. But there is something I have been meaning to ask you and it relates to Imran. Think about what I'm about to ask as part of your comradely duty...'

Knowing what was to come Verity looked at the captain who obviously knew too, and she felt something give inside her.

'What more do you want from me Tariq? I'm already busy with the activist stuff, teaching night school, and what I do for the underground, not to mention trying to hold down a full-time job and study.'

'Imran is lonely. He needs comfort...being on the Island all that time...you know...celibate. Try and imagine what it's been like for him, all those years behind bars, then years in exile or on the run. It isn't natural.'

'No Tariq! You bastard! Not that!'

'Shhh, baby, he'll hear you. Don't get so upset.'

'You're telling me that the idea of your handler fucking me doesn't upset you?'

'He's not my handler…and it's for the cause.'

'Not my fucking cause! Jesus Tariq!'

'I'm just doing what the leadership have asked of me.'

'Fuck the leadership. Is their next directive to the women's movement that we all get on our backs? I suppose it'll make a change from us doing the singing and dancing at conferences where men do all the talking.'

At this the captain laughed.

On the tape came the sound of a door slamming.

'Verity, come back. Don't do it for the leadership then, or even for Imran, do it for me. I'll love you all more for it.'

The sound of a door opening, footsteps, the creak of bed springs.

Verity felt two pairs of eyes boring into her as blood infused her shamed cheeks.

'If I do this now, say you'll never ask me to do anything like this ever again.'

'I promise, baby, just this once. Afterwards we'll make other arrangements for him.'

'For Christ's sake Tariq, have they got you pimping for the struggle now?'

'Don't be silly. You know this will make you a soldier for Umkhonto weSizwe, the Spear of our Nation.'

'A spear through my heart, Tariq, that's what it will be, a spear through my heart.'

The young officer pressed stop and began to remove the reel. 'Shall I get the next one ready, Kaptein,' he asked.

'No. I think we've given Verity enough to ponder on for one day, don't you?'

Walking back to her cell Verity tasted bile rising in her throat. Keeping her arms folded over her breasts, she tried to ignore the uniformed officer, thankful he had not been party to her humiliation over Imran. How could she have let herself do such a thing? Hearing the conversation on the tape made it seem even worse than it had seemed at the time. As soon as she was alone in her cell she threw up. She wiped her mouth with the back of her hand and lay down on the mattress on the floor. It was dusk now and insects had begun to gather around the light of the bare bulb. Hearing the whine of a mosquito around her head she swatted at her neck. As she felt the slap of her palm against her skin, she remembered Tariq swatting at mosquitoes in the Drakensberg and how much he had said he loved her.

*   *   *

They had gone wild camping in the mountains in a borrowed tent. It had been warm and they had lain on top of a single sleeping bag looking at the night sky through the unzipped opening of the tent.

'Listen, can you hear the nightjar?' Tariq had asked.

'No, I can only hear the drone of that damned mosquito that's been biting you.'

'Verity,' he said, kneeling up, his shoe in his hand, 'I'm going to have to ignore what your yoga teacher tells you about honouring all life.'

'No,' she had cried.

'Too late!' The corners of his mouth lifted as he stretched for the black spot on the canvas. 'See, I've swatted the bloody thing!'

He flopped back down, his black hair falling heavy and long over his face.

'The world can live without one more mosquito my Verity,' he had said, pulling her on top of him, 'but I cannot live without you.'

Those camping trips had become a regular occurrence for them, the only place they could be alone, the place where Tariq always professed his love for her, and she could uninhibitedly savour the very feel of him.

Verity had pursued Tariq relentlessly and eventually he had succumbed. Her first gambit had been to ask her boss if she could watch a baby being delivered.

'I don't see why not although a Caesarean Section would be more predictable. You're a bright girl, Verity,' Professor Sithole had said, 'and I know you'll move on from this job in due course. It's in my interest to keep you stimulated for as long as possible.'

Verity knew she would have to stand next to the anaesthetist, and she had contrived for that anaesthetist to be Tariq. Gowned and sterilised, she had stood beside him as he explained to the woman on the operating table that she would have an injection and go to sleep and that when she woke up it would all be over.

'Florence Mkhize,' he said kindly, checking the name on her wristband. 'Do you understand my sister?'

Verity's eyes moved between the mother's trusting face and her mountainous belly protruding from the green drapes. At the first incision she swayed. With the sound of the second into the uterus wall, she'd had to hold on to a trolley. When a pinkish-grey, squirming body emerged, and the baby cried, a congratulatory murmur echoed around the theatre.

'We do this day in and day out but every time it feels like a wonder,' Professor Sithole said. 'Verity, do you know why we had to get the little chap out so quickly?'

'Does the mother have pre-eclampsia?'

'Quite right. See Randeree, she doesn't just type up my notes, she reads and understands them. She's wasted behind a typewriter in my view, but for now I just count my lucky stars.'

'He is a real charmer and gets all the girls. I just put them to sleep,' Tariq said to Verity with a grin. 'When she wakes up, Florence Mkhize will only remember the Professor.'

'My magnetic charm,' said the obstetrician, pinging off his surgical gloves.

After the procedure had finished, Verity waited for Tariq and they fell into step as they made their way back to the medical school, where he steered her into the doctor's canteen. It was a place where black, brown and white medics ate and drank together behind closed doors, their shared professional status quietly trumping Apartheid's segregationist laws.

'Is it true that Florence Mkhize won't remember you?' Verity asked as they queued for tea.

'I was just ribbing Sithole, but it is a fact that her memory of me will be more vague.'

'Do you mind?'

'Not at all. I prefer to work behind the scenes.'

They found a space to one side of the canteen and sat at a Formica table.

'If you're as bright as Sithole says, why aren't you furthering your education?'

'I am. I study part-time at the campus up the hill. I chose to work here so I can get the staff fee waiver.'

'Oh, you can do that?'

'Yes, administratively we're all one university even though the different campuses are segregated. I thought this job would be more interesting than the other on offer at the business school.'

'And you have no problem working for a black boss?'

'Not at all, and the job's really interesting.'

'What about missing out on the fun and games of normal campus life?'

'You can't have everything and I wanted to pay my own way. My father died not so long ago and my mother and I don't always see eye to eye.'

'I'm sorry.' Tariq fastidiously removed a tea leaf floating in his mug with a neat, buffed fingernail. 'About your father's death I mean.'

'Thank you.'

'Did the sight of blood make you feel faint today? I saw you gripping the trolley.'

'No, I just felt dizzy from watching you. You see, I really like you. Do you like me?'

'You obviously care about things, and as Sithole says, you're intelligent.' His tone was dismissive and curt.

'What about in other ways?' she persisted.

'Other ways are irrelevant,' he said with dry impatience. 'You're young, white, and extremely naïve.' He was silent after that, staring hard-faced into his mug.

Verity realising she had overstepped the mark, stood up, embarrassed, and in her haste she knocked the table, sending ripples across her unfinished tea.

In the end she had worn him down though. One day she had found a note under the hood of her typewriter from Tariq requesting her assistance in the Gestetner room. She sighed at the thought of more illicit printing, and when he locked the door behind them she thought the pamphlet must be hot stuff, but instead he pulled her in close and kissed her long and hard.

'What took you so long?' she'd asked.

'I'm nearly fifteen years your senior and, in case you hadn't noticed, I'm Indian. You are white, so what we are doing right now is essentially illegal.'

'I don't care,' she had said, her keening excitement having as much to do with the illicit nature of what they were doing as the thrill of his body against hers.

Outwardly, little shifted at first. They talked endlessly about politics and engaged in activism, but never exchanged meaningful glances in public. They couldn't go to movies, restaurants, bars, or clubs together. Every venue was delineated by race. The beaches were segregated, even watching cricket was off limits because the stadiums had separate sections. And that was when they found their love of camping, their safe space up in the mountains where they could finally be together.

'Have you done this before?' Tariq asked, the first time they made love.

'Not exactly,' she said.

'What then, exactly?' He said with a hint of amusement.

She told him about cramped fumbles with boyfriends in the back seats of cars, but did not elaborate on how the coach of the Marist Brothers' debating team had inducted her into the pleasurable mechanics of non-penetrative sex, before heading off to the priesthood in a flurry of self-denial. It was not long though before Tariq took Verity to places her tormented Catholic debating coach could only have imagined.

A few weeks after their first night under canvas, in the airless Gestetner room, Tariq had traced a thumb across a brown stain on Verity's upper lip.

'What's this?'

'You're getting under my skin,' she laughed.

'It's not funny. It is melasma, a side effect of the pill.'

'A rep who visits the department gave me samples. I thought it would be good to be prepared.' Her words met the steel face of his displeasure.

'We should have talked about it, don't you think? It's obviously not the right one for you.'

Tariq gave her a prescription for another brand, the blotches cleared up and Verity was more convinced than ever that with him, she was in safe hands. They grew closer and when the camping trips were no longer enough they decided to simply brazen it out and get an apartment together. The lease was in Verity's name because it was in a white area, but as the higher earner Tariq had paid the lion's share of the rent.

They found joy in simply being together and doing ordinary things, like cooking, yoga, listening to music and Tariq loved to regale her with the poems of his favourite Sufi poet, Mirza Ghalib.

'Here, listen to this one, Verity. 'Drunk on love, I made her my God. She quickly informed me God belongs to no man!'

'Sounds like a sensible fellow your Ghalib.'

On their first night together in their plain pine double bed, she had found on her pillow a translation of another Ghalib poem. She knew it now by heart.

Let's live in that place where there's no one, let's go,
Where no one knows our tongue, there's no one to speak to.
We'd build a house without doors and walls,
Have no neighbours, watchmen forego.

*   *   *

These recollections compelled Verity to a tenderness she wished she could bottle, knowing only too well that it could be obliterated in a moment, leaving in its place a terror that could rumble through her like a Drakensberg thunderstorm.

6

Verity was awake and sitting on the mattress when breakfast was brought in. It was the two boys this time and they offered no salute. She ate and then returned to the commandments in an effort to keep her mind from straying towards Tariq. Commandment Three: comrades should keep themselves clean.

She hadn't showered since that first humiliation. She had changed her underwear, and quickly washed between her legs and under her arms, but she could still smell the mixture of stale sweat and carbolic soap on her clothes, an odour she decided she would rather put up with than risk being naked and exposed in the courtyard. If she couldn't properly clean herself, she thought, she could at least try and clean the cell.

She looked over to the calendar of faeces on the wall by the toilet and remembered the box of sanitary pads the female warder had given her. As she had no use for them, she thought she may as well try and use them to clean the wall. Damping down one of the pads in the toilet water, she began to scrub the wall. The addition of water to the lines of excrement brought the smell alive and Verity retched. She rubbed until the pad was a mess of shredded, shit-stained cotton, then she put it in the toilet and flushed, having to force it through the bend with her arm. She took another pad from the box and repeated the process, but the pads were not up to the job. The marks had faded but there was still the trenchant smell of someone else's shit.

Verity gave up, went out into the courtyard and lathering up her hands and arms in carbolic soap she scrubbed and scrubbed under the shower until she convinced herself there was no trace of her recent activity left on her skin. Back in her cell she sat on the wedge wondering what to do next. The door opened and a neatly dressed man, with a short-sleeved khaki shirt and brown tie, walked in carrying a clipboard. He didn't speak, just looked around the cell and made some notes on his form.

'Any complaints?' he asked, when he had finished writing.

'What?'

'Any complaints?' he repeated, looking at Verity as if she was deliberately trying to test his patience.

'Yes,' she said, rallying. 'I'm being held without charge. I want to be charged or released.'

'Take that up with the security branch.'

'One of the uniformed officers barged in when I was having a shower, and he's rough with me when he takes me upstairs for interrogation.'

'I'll pass it on, but that's also for the security police.'

'What am I supposed to complain to you about then?'

'Your conditions. We're obliged to report to the International Red Cross on the condition of all political prisoners. They seem to think they have the right to interfere in the internal affairs of our country.'

'Well, I'm glad someone does.'

'And before you start, you politicals already get better food than common law prisoners and whites are better off than black inmates. Anything else?'

'Toilet paper. They only gave me one roll and it's nearly finished.'

He slowly wrote toilet paper in large capitals on his form, then looked up, pen poised.

'And cleaning materials; a scrubbing brush, maybe some Handy Andy,' said Verity thinking back to the marks on the wall by the toilet.

'I doubt the International Red Cross will be interested in Handy Andy, and it's not on the checklist.' He clicked his ball point closed and left.

As the door shut behind him, Verity remembered the three-legged bed.

'And a bed, I need a new bed,' she shouted in a voice too thin and too late.

Shortly after the man had left, lunch arrived. It was the usual fare, which Verity forced down because of the child growing inside her. When she had finished her hands strayed protectively to her stomach, and she was unable to prevent her thoughts from turning to Tariq and wondering where he was. She took the tampon from her spongebag, and carefully unpeeled the wrapper, gently pulling the fine paper note until she was able to extract it from the tube. She unfolded it and traced her fingers over the imprint of Tariq's small, neat hand.

I am left with no hope at all,
No possibility to reach my goal,

The day of my death is fixed,
I am so very anxious that I cannot sleep all night.
Though I know the reward of obedience and worship,
But I have no tendency for it.
I am silent for a certain reason,
Otherwise I can convince you with my words,
Why I shouldn't cry,
For when I don't, she asks about me,
My heart is burning, though you cannot see the spot,
But O my doctor, can't you smell my heart burn?

He had carefully transcribed this verse by Mirza Ghalib, and she read it over and over, trying to decipher its meaning, searching for clues, or hidden messages. He was afraid. Of course he was, but what did he mean by the line, I am left with no hope at all? Why had he sent the note ahead via room service? Had he thought he might not be able to say goodbye to her in person? Did he think she would buckle under interrogation? No, she thought, his last words had been to call her a warrior. Verity's confusion stretched into anger. I am so very anxious that I cannot sleep all night. Well, you're not the only one. I was the sodding decoy, and I'm the one now in prison.

The day slipped by and still Verity ran the words over in her head. Supper arrived and again Verity forced down the pap. When she had finished, she lay back on the mattress and continued to scrutinise the paper, looking for something she may have missed. Defeated, she squeezed the note into a small slit in the mattress and closed her eyes against the glare of the bulb, longing for lights out. When it came she heard the sound of a key in the lock and sat upright in fright.

'Hurry up you bitch. I has got a surprise for you tonight.' The uniformed officer stood holding open the door.

Verity followed him down the corridor and waited for the grip on her arm, but it didn't come. He walked ahead, constantly looking back at her, telling her to hurry along.

'You think it's okay to cheek me, you bitch,' he said as soon as the elevator door closed behind them, prodding her buttocks with his baton.

On the seventh floor he steered her not towards the usual interrogation space but to a smaller room that smelt of urine and stale cigarette smoke. Inside the young officer with acne who Verity had dubbed the Tapeworm, was setting up the machine on a table in the corner.

'Where's the captain?' Verity asked.

'He's on mission and I'm in charge tonight,' said the uniformed officer, as he pointed with his baton to a brick on the floor.

'Verity stared at it, wondering what she was supposed to do with it.

'Stand on it,' he barked.

Verity lifted one foot and then the other and raised herself up on the brick, relying on the balls of her feet to keep her balanced. It was not long before she felt the burn in the muscles of her calves.

'Okay, let's get this fokking show on the road.'

The young officer started up the tape machine and the officer with the baton leant back against the wall, a cigarette gripped between nicotine-stained fingers. The reels turned and the tape hissed to life.

'She's just a working-class tart who couldn't attract a white doctor, so got her claws into my Tariq.'

It was the voice of Tariq's mother.

'Maybe you should just accept that they're in love,' came the voice of her sister, Ma. 'Verity is a lovely young woman, and she is Yasmin's good friend. Anyway, they're already living together.'

'She is no good for him. He could do so much better for himself. I just hope he's using her until the new law comes in. Then we'll be able to buy property in white areas ourselves. After that he'll have no need of her.'

The tape clicked to a halt.

'Ja, you see, these fokking coolies! They can't wait to take over and get their hands on our houses,' said the uniformed officer, pounding the table with his baton.

Verity could barely concentrate because of her trembling calves and aching lower back. She wondered if she should tell them she was pregnant but thought better of it, knowing they would only use it against her.

'I is looking forward to the next one, quick, play the blerrie thing, seuntjie.'

'Then no more after,' said the Tapeworm, looking anxiously at his watch and then at Verity.

The next voice the magnetic tape delivered into the room was Tariq's.

'I love the feel of those soft round breasts of yours.'

The Tapeworm grunted in satisfaction. Verity looked at him in disgust. His face no longer looked childish to her, but cruel.

'I didn't know it could be like that Tariq. I've kissed guys before but haven't been with a man properly until now.'

It was a woman's voice; a voice Verity didn't recognise.

'I aim to please, my little love kitten,' said Tariq and the sound of his familiar chuckle made Verity feel sick. 'When you're on the pill we'll do it properly. I'll show you next time how to pleasure me.'

'Oh, I want to, when?'

Tariq's betrayal detonated inside Verity's brain, exploding again and again.

'Ja Juffrou, how often do you think they is doing it behind your back? Was this recorded in your apartment I wonder? Or does he bring his dirty underpants for you to wash when he's left her at his mother's place? Play that last tape again seuntjie, I want to see Juffrou Saunders squirm.'

Verity swayed as the same conversation filled the room. In her head she screamed, 'fuck your little love kitten', and 'what about me, what about our baby?'

'Weer, seuntjie.'

'I think that's enough Sergeant Swart,' the young officer said, looking at his watch again. 'We'll get in trouble.'

On hearing the officer's name Verity wobbled on the brick and let out a choked cry. The man with the baton who had been terrorising her, was the infamous Kobus Swart. He was the torturer whose reputation for cruelty preceded him, who had hurt and harmed Tariq beyond belief.

'I could have told you not to trust a fokking coolie,' Swart said to Verity.

'Tariq's a respected doctor who heals people, he doesn't hurt them like you.' She clenched and unclenched her fists as she struggled for balance.

'Nee, Juffrou, he's just a slimy coolie, worse than a black.' Swart pushed his stocky bulk from the wall and gripped her shoulders.

'Get away from me, you disgusting fuck,' she shouted as he brought his ruddy face up close to hers.

He struck her hard across the face, his gold and onyx ring lancing her cheek. Verity fell to the floor, then struggled to her feet, but he threw her against the door. A she clawed herself up by the frame, Swart grabbed her by the hair and hit her head hard against the wall. He unclipped the baton from his waist and when the blow came it landed hard on her shoulder. She sank to the floor.

'Meneer,' said the young officer, 'enough already. We're not even supposed to be here.'

'Shut up seuntjie.'

'She's white, Sergeant, and she's British. She could report you.'

'She's nothing but a coolie cocksucker,' Swart said, flushed with loathing.

'The captain will hear about this,' Verity said, avoiding both their eyes.

'He isn't back for a long time, and you is going back to your cell for even longer. Tonight, you better think of Imran Malik as you rub your little cunt in bed, because your coolie doctor is gone to Amira.'

7

Movement and thought both hurt. Verity tried to stretch but arching her back was painful. Her calves ached from balancing on the upturned brick and her head hurt where Swart had hit it against the wall. Inside her chest a pressure began to build. Swart, the very name Tariq had been reluctant to share with her, the very man who had hurt him so badly. It was Yasmin who had eventually told Verity what the sergeant had done. She cast her mind back to the day Tariq had been released from prison.

*　　　　　*　　　　　*

It had been a slow day at work when Verity had picked up the phone to Yasmin's breathless voice.

'He's out Verity...they've finally released him. They dropped him off at his mother's place. I picked him up and took him home. He's there now.'

Verity had put down the receiver and rushed back to the

apartment to find Tariq sitting in an armchair staring into space. She ran to him, straddled his lap, flung her arms around his neck and kissed his face. He flinched and turned away from her. She pulled him up from the chair and unbuttoned his shirt, her fingers seeking the familiar smattering of hair down his sternum. The feel of scar tissue stopped her in her tracks. He stood mute as she peeled off his shirt, walked around him, and traced the palm of her hand over the rough, raised stripes across his back.

'Oh Tariq, they really hurt you,' she said, hanging her head. He hung his too and they both stood facing each other, staring at the floor. 'Tell me what happened. Who did this to you, my love?'

'You don't need to know Verity,' he said in a tired voice. 'I don't want to talk about it.'

'But they beat you Tariq. The evidence is on your body,' she insisted.

'It is true they were brutal,' he said quietly, 'but it was the malice that was the most frightening of all.'

Those were Tariq's last words on the matter. He slid into a remote and unreachable world governed by ever shifting rules of silence. He no longer enjoyed the routines of domestic life, or the comforts of their bed. He prowled restlessly from room to room, often retreating to his mother's place. Trying to comprehend what had happened to him, Verity turned to Yasmin.

'He won't even talk to me Yas,' Verity pleaded. 'He won't make love and if it happens at all, it ends badly. He avoids even lying in bed with me.'

'I guess it's time that I told you what they did to him. Tariq wanted to protect you from it all, but I think it's best you know. A sadistic cop called Kobus Swart whipped him across the back and chest, and applied electrodes to Tariq's genitals to make him talk. When Tariq refused, and somehow he managed to hold out...I don't know how...Swart inserted a live cattle prod in his anus.'

Verity had cried out against the image and her own foolish ignorance. Yasmin advised her to give Tariq time, to wait for him to come round, and not to pressure him, but weeks and months passed and he never returned to the man he was before. Always at home with his body, Tariq used to do morning yoga naked, but not after Swart. He no longer ate his breakfast shirtless with just a lungi around his waist, and the smile she had loved so much had all but disappeared, along with any kind of intimacy. Eventually Verity stopped bothering to take her contraceptive pill, thinking there was no point filling herself with hormones for no reason.

They continued to share their work as activists and pursued their respective underground activities, with Tariq now spending long and unexplained periods away from home. As disciplined comrades, they rarely discussed what they were up to, and never asked each other, but this only served to increase the yawning distance growing between them. In the mornings, Verity would watch him through half-closed eyes as he dressed rapidly, wondering if danger and intrigue provided him with the edge he needed in his life, a danger that simply left her exhausted.

Then one night after a long absence away, Verity had woken to find Tariq leaning on his elbow looking at her. He said he had been told to pass on the leadership's appreciation for her recent contribution to the struggle, which they had noted as both important and brave. It had not felt particularly significant at the time, just another courier visit to London carrying some sort of information for the ANC, concealed in a tube of toothpaste. She had handed it over at a pre-arranged brush-by at the Burger King in Kings Cross Station on a grey and rainy afternoon, to the only black guy in the place with a copy of *Time Out* sticking out of his jacket pocket.

That night they lay in bed together with arms around each other in a circle of warmth until Verity tentatively reached out to him. This time he responded. Their lovemaking was tender, a desperate attempt to show each other care at the tail-end of bone-deep anxiety and exhaustion. Six weeks later Verity told Tariq she was pregnant.

He had been thrilled and shared their news with Professor Sithole who was keen to demonstrate his new state-of-the-art ultrasound machine, one of the first in the country. As he moved the probe across Verity's stomach and they saw the grainy pulsating image of a heartbeat on the screen, shallow breaths from Tariq's open mouth brushed against Verity's cheek.

'That's our baby,' he whispered, his voice uneven with emotion.

Verity went with Professor Sithole to print off a copy of the scan and when she returned she found Tariq rocking back and forth on the floor, muttering under his breath. She realised he was praying, strings of words repeated until a rasp in his throat replaced all speech. Seeing her he stood up and put his hands on her shoulders.

'We will love this child, Verity, with all our hearts, and we will continue our fight for a world in which all children will grow up equal and loved.'

*   *   *

Verity got up from the mattress, physical pain shooting through her body, matching the pain she felt in her heart. How could the man that she had seen praying so fervently for their unborn child, the man who had declared that he loved her from the depths of his being, be the same man she had heard on the tape talking to a girl called Amira. Was she the girl Mrs Randeree was trying to arrange for him to marry?. Had his mother been right all along, saying that he only stayed with Verity because he found the apartment too convenient to give up? Where did that leave the two of them as budding parents?

Verity ran over the words of the Ghalib poem he had transcribed in his last note. My heart is burning, though you cannot see the spot. Yeah, right, she thought, fear and fury scuttling across her brain. Who is it that your heart is burning for, you bastard? If your heart is burning, then mine is frigging breaking.

8

During the night, Verity had struggled to find comfort. The bruises on her body hurt like hell and thoughts of Tariq tore at her emotions. As she listened to the nightshift handing over to the day staff, she heard a twist in the lock of the courtyard door. She feared that it signalled the arrival of Kobus Swart, and wished they would just leave her alone for one day. Her breath came fast with the anxiety that accompanied anticipation of interrogation, but it was a softer male voice who was calling her name.

'Virity, Virity?'

She held her breath and waited before venturing into the courtyard, where she saw a young, blond officer standing at the gate. He had a baby-face that seemed out of place in a police uniform and a sparse moustache dusted his upper lip.

'Hello,' he said. 'You must be Virity?'

'Verity, yes.'

'That's what I said,' he insisted in his thick Afrikaans accent. 'I came to see how you are, to see if there's anything you need?'

'Who sent you? Who are you?'

'No one. Just call me Jan Niemand.'

'That means John Nobody.'

'Correct. Don't worry, I'm here to help. If there's something you need, within reason of course, I'll try and get it.' He offered her a lopsided grin.

For reasons she did not try to fathom, Verity avoided her usual spiel about wanting to be charged or released. Perhaps the message was beginning to seep in that constantly rocking the boat didn't help her.

'A new bed would be good, this one only has three legs...' and then remembering the note she had hidden, added, 'but the mattress is good. I can keep that.'

Jan Niemand called out to one of the black workers who came in from the corridor. 'Get rid of that frame and fetch a new one,' he said, unlocking the gate for him. 'One with all of its legs this time.'

Verity stepped aside as the guard dragged the frame from the cell.

'Anything else?'

'Perhaps another sheet and a pillow. The cover is ripped and what's left of the feathers keep falling out. They set off my allergies.'

'Ja, I see. Problem is prisoners keep their contraband in the pillows. There are none left in the storeroom. Seems to be quite a busy time for us here at present. Lots of comings and goings. Hard to keep track of what's happening. Did you have an interrogation last night?'

'I did,' Verity said hesitantly.

'Hmm,' he murmured, glancing at the bruises on her arm.

Verity wondered if he had been sent to play good cop to Kobus

Swart's bad one. She knew they did that, to mess with your head and break down your defences. The officer looked at her intently and she thought he was about to say something, but just then the worker returned with the new bed and another sheet, which he dumped in the cell.

'Vasbyt,' Jan Niemand said and with the loose lift of a hand, he was gone.

Verity pulled the mattress onto the frame and lay down. The bed creaked beneath her but at least it was stable. She thought that perhaps tonight she might get some sleep, but now was not the time. Despite the lure of more comfortable sleeping arrangements, lying around feeling sorry for herself was not an option. She had another whole day to get through and they could come for her again at any moment, so she began her exercise routine around the courtyard. As she paced she ran the through the events of the previous night, hoping the tape she had heard had somehow been faked.

As she walked, she could smell her own body odour coming from herself and from her clothes. She paused and glanced around. All was quiet no sounds from the other prisoners, no sounds coming from the corridors. She quickly undressed and ducked under the cold water, running a hand over her stomach, which was beginning to swell. She carefully moved the carbolic soap over the bruises on her arms and winced as it touched the welt on her shoulder. Then, as if on cue the courtyard door opened. This time it was the Tapeworm who stood at the gate.

'Get a life,' Verity said wearily as she rapidly pulled on her T-shirt over her wet body.

'Sorry,' he stammered, and he quickly backed away, closing the door behind him.

Once she was certain he had gone, Verity went back into her

cell and pulled on the only clean top she had, then returned to the courtyard to scrub down her clothes. The soap was by now only a slither, but she couldn't delay washing her stuff any longer. She sloshed her underwear, pyjamas, T-shirts and joggers under the shower, then set to work scrubbing them. She rinsed them off under the spout, wrung them out as best she could and as she watched the soapy water drain away, an image came to her of Gladys, her blue maid's uniform moving audibly as she slapped suds-filled clothes against the washboard over her mother's kitchen sink.

*   *   *

The last time Verity had seen Gladys was also the last time she had seen her mother and sister. Visiting after a long absence and following the fractious Christmas dinner they had shared, Verity had gone through to the kitchen to give Gladys a hug, resting her head on the familiar comfort of the span of her bosom.

'Nkosazane, I am worried for you. I think enough of politics now. No more, okay?' Gladys patted her former charge as if burping a baby.

'And enough of Nkosazane!' Verity retorted with a grin. 'I'm not your little princess.'

'But you're still my child. I know what goes on in the townships. These young lions, they don't listen to their mothers anymore and not all those who call themselves comrades are good ones.'

'Don't worry Glad. My comrades are good ones.'

'Maybe, Miss Verity,' Gladys had said, but she did not look convinced.

When she brought through the tray of tea, she placed a large slice of lemon drizzle cake by Verity's chair.

'I baked your favourite, Nkosazane.'

'Do you think you should, dear?' said her mother, 'I see signs of a muffin top. Don't encourage her Gladys.'

'Give it a rest Mum, can't you?'

Her mother reached for the silver sugar tongs, gripped a single cube in the talons and dropped it deliberately in her tea. Gladys raised a private eyebrow in Verity's direction and retreated. The silence that followed was only broken by the scraping of silver forks on china plates until the welcome arrival of Louise.

'Hello, my Lou-Lou,' their mother said, offering her younger daughter her cheek.

'Hi Mave.' Louise kissed her mother and flopped into a chair, kicking off her sandals and draping her long, tanned legs over one of the arms. 'Howzit, V?'

'All good,' said Verity, feeling a rush of affection for her younger sister. She got up to fetch Louise another teacup, before Mavis could ring the embarrassing little silver bell that she used to summon Gladys, and she ruffled her sister's hair as she passed.

When she returned she found Mavis and Louise deep in conversation about who they had been drawn to play in the women's doubles tournament at the tennis club. Verity watched the easy knowing between them with a twinge of envy. Before her father died their nuclear unit had felt sturdy and strong and he had always stood as a protective barrier between Verity and her mother's acerbic tongue. Verity felt that her mother's mourning had left no room for her own, and she withdrew away from most family interaction, taking her own grief elsewhere. In her absence Louise had rallied, behaving more like the older than the younger sibling, taking on the mantle of family conciliator.

Waiting for their conversation to finish, Verity looked around at the family house, all chintz and oak, brass and copper. It was middle England transported to the tropics, nostalgia with sunshine and servants attached. This is no longer my home, she thought. It's not even my country.

'Your sister has been such a blessing to me, Verity. I don't know what I would have done without her. Do you know that people talk behind my back about you cavorting with an Indian. I hear them at the hairdressers when I'm under the drier. It's so humiliating.' Mavis lit a cigarette, exhaling a stream of grey tendrils that encircled her perm.

To avoid rising to her mother's bait, Verity went through to the bathroom and looked at herself in the full-length mirror. Her frame was sturdy and her leg and arm muscles were toned. There was no visible thickening around her waist, it was too early for that, but she thought that if her mother mentioned it again, she would admit to having a muffin top, because now was not the time to tell her she was going to be a grandmother.

'What have you been up to, Lou, painting the town red?' Verity asked when she returned to join her mother and sister, determined to try and keep things light.

'Nothing much. The only thing I paint red right now are my toenails.' She stuck out her bare feet for inspection. 'I spend all my time on lesson prep and have so much marking, I've no time to jorl.'

'All work and no play makes for a dull girl, Lou-Lou,' said their mother, 'at this rate you'll never find a boyfriend, and that short cropped haircut doesn't help.'

Verity wondered when her mother would cotton on to the fact that her favourite daughter was a lesbian.

'Not that it's very safe to go into town now though, what with the riots and the blacks causing even more trouble, continued their mother, 'with all the unrest in the townships I even wonder how much longer I can trust Gladys before she turns on me.'

'Mave! How can you say that?' said Louise. 'She's worked for our family for over twenty years.'

At that moment Gladys walked into the room and as she loaded the tray with cups and plates, Verity wondered if she had overheard the last exchange. Her bearing gave nothing away, but when Mavis acknowledged the delicious cake she made, she had said 'thank you M'am' without looking up from the tray, with more of an emphasis on the M'am than usual.

When Verity left, Lou followed her to the car and gave her a squeeze. 'Thanks for biting your tongue back there. I really wasn't up for another Saunders women fracas this afternoon. Last Christmas was bad enough.'

*   *   *

Verity gathered up her newly washed clothes from the courtyard floor and held them close to her face, inhaling the carbolic whiff that permeated. How she wished she could replace it with Louise's basic, no-nonsense Palmolive Milk and Honey. As she savoured the recollection of that last hug from her sister before she was arrested, she was overcome and gave in to a great heaving sob.

9

Verity had long since lost track of the passing days and wondered why no one had been back in to take her for interrogation. There had been no more visits from Swart and after a couple of brief visits, Jan Niemand had not been back to see her. Perhaps they had no more use for her, she thought. Perhaps they had forgotten about her. She languished through long days of anxious waiting and nothingness, and spent hours lying listlessly on her bed, her nights disoriented by heat and dreams.

The cool, dry days of Durban's winter had passed, when she could distinguish morning from afternoon by the slant of the sunlight across the courtyard, tracing the shadows as they moved across the concrete floor and walls. Now it was hot and humid and for the last few days, a choleric sub-tropical sky had poured angry rain into the courtyard, leaving puddles in the dips and craters of the rough-thrown floor. Everything felt permanently damp, including everyone's mood. Fury sounded through walls and doors. Fed-up prisoners shouted angry demands, and impatient guards stomped down corridors, banging their batons against cell doors.

Verity lay on the bed examining the hairs on her arms, running her fingers over the downy blonde, noticing how her tan had completely faded. She pulled individual hairs from her shins, a pointless effort at personal grooming but one that helped relieve the boredom. On the wall she watched a daddy-long-legs as it would ascend a few inches then fall back, before trying again. Verity stood on the toilet, pulled herself onto the half-wall beside it, and cupped the creature in her hands. She released it onto the window ledge near a torn piece in the mesh covering. She waited. It remained tightly curled then slowly, accepting it was safe, it released its fragile legs and scuttled away.

Her ear then settled on the sound of a squeaky trolley wheel in the corridor outside. Verity had never been so alert to sounds as she was now. She tried to conjure up happier sounds, the ones she used to take for granted, like the shrill three-note call of hadeda ibises on their morning flights from their nests, or the rustle of strelitzia leaves outside her office window. She thought about the whistling cough of her colleague in the office next to hers as he packed his satchel at the end of the day, and the call of the mynah birds in the trees near where she parked her car. To be sequestered in the white female section of an apartheid jail was to be as far away from other prisoners as it was possible to be, but sound travelled, and no one had prepared her for how loud solitary confinement could be. Distant calls, angry shouts, occasional laughter, the unrelenting moans of anguish and longing, the emotions of people she would never know.

One night she heard a bloodcurdling scream from somewhere very close. It came again, then another and another, each time louder, and more desperate.

'Please no. Please no baas.' It was a young Zulu voice, perhaps even that of a boy, pleading for mercy in English.

'Shut the fok up and suck his dick or we is all going to have you.'

Verity pulled the pillow over her head in a vain attempt to block them out, but the cries and grunts kept coming. How long they continued she did not know but in the depths of the night, when all else was quiet she heard a stifled whimpering from the cell next to hers.

Early the following morning a familiar face called for her from the courtyard gate.

'How are you Virity?' It was Jan Niemand. 'I thought I would come and check all is okay with you?'

'Where have you been?'

'They've been keeping me busy upstairs. I have lots of things to do other than looking out for you, you know, Virity. How was breakfast?'

'As you might imagine. You should try it sometime.'

'The jacarandas are out. Some of the roads in Durban are completely covered in purple flowers. Do you like jacaranda season, Virity?'

Verity sensed that his polite enquires were leading up to something else.

'I understand it was quite a busy night in here last night. I just wanted to see how you were doing?'

'It was horrible. Did you know about it?'

'I heard this morning that something irregular happened. Some of the prison warders can get out of hand. I mean the prisoners do provoke them but there's a few of them who treat this place as if it's their own little kingdom. Are you okay?'

'Why do you care? Why do you bother coming to visit me?'

'I'm just checking, that's all.'

'Why me? Do you check on everyone? How come you even knew I was in here in the first place?'

'I hear things on the grapevine, and there are not that many white politicals. I told my mother about you, and she said I should be kind to you.'

'Why, because I'm white?'

He looked at her quizzically, and although Verity did not want to admit it to herself, she had missed his visits. He was the only person she could have a normal conversation with, or as normal as one could get in a place like this. Still, she reminded herself, Jan Niemand was with the police, maybe even the security police, so as much as she might want him to be her good Samaritan, she could never let her guard down.

'Why are they ignoring me?'

'Who?'

'Come on John Nobody, I haven't been interrogated for ages. No one comes for me anymore.'

'Ja, well isn't that good? You must be feeling a bit more relaxed.'

Verity let out a disbelieving snigger.

'I must get going. Is there anything else you need?'

'I'm curious as to why they take the handles of the mugs?'

'You know what curiosity did to the cat?'

'I heard,' she said relenting and smiled.

'Actually, it's because if they don't, prisoners remove them and sharpen them up, to use in fights or to cut themselves, you know, suicide. We must make sure everyone stays safe.'

The following day dawned eerily quiet. The low-grade anger of the prison seemed to have dissipated. The unrelenting cacophony had not just paused but had ceased completely. The silence was absolute, pregnant with impossibility.

Verity did her usual circuits around the courtyard and then sat in her favoured position on the doorstep between her cell and the courtyard, watching the early morning sun burn off the grey, creating scatterings of light in the puddles left over from the previous night's rain. Breakfast was late and when it came it was delivered by a strange face. Alongside the usual enamel dish of pap were two slices of buttered bread, a can of soda and a packet of crisps.

'What's this in aid of?' Verity asked.

'It's Christmas,' said the unfamiliar woman over her shoulder on her way out.

Verity opened the can and took a sip. The soda was warm but tasted sweet. She put it to one side, to make it last the whole day. She opened the crisps and put one in her mouth but spat it out. After so long without salt her taste buds revolted against the artificial sodium tang, and she turned to the familiar mealie pap with its crust of sugar and sank in her balsawood spoon.

After eating she dawdled her way through the morning picking lice from her scalp. One by one she buried them in a broken off corner of carbolic soap. Her head was crawling, so it was a fool's errand, but it gave her something vaguely useful to do.

Lunch came early, the usual enamel bowl of pap, but swimming in a thick gravy that contained meat. She fell upon it, chewing vigorously until only a row of indigestible bones lay clean on a corner of the tray. Clinging tightly to the empty bowl she made aimless patterns with her finger in the last trace of gravy at its bottom, wondering what her mother and sister would be doing now. Mavis would be on the telephone making overseas calls to British relatives wishing them happy Christmas and moaning about the heat. Louise would probably be decorating the table, trying to ensure, for her mother's sake, that tradition and some kind of normality was maintained, despite the fact that this year it would just be the two of them.

*   *   *

Their last Christmas together had been an absolute nightmare. Verity had begged Tariq to join them. He eventually agreed, both against his better judgement and Mavis's wishes, and it had turned out to be a huge mistake.

'Verity, Mavis really doesn't want me there and I feel uncomfortable about the whole thing, especially the emphasis you all put on exchanging gifts. At Eid we just give the young ones some money and they get themselves what they want. I have no idea what to give your mother or your sister.'

'Anything's fine, it's just a gesture,' Verity insisted. 'I've told you Mum always goes over the top but that's just how she is, we don't have to match her. Some bath salts, or scented soap will be fine.'

In the event, her mother had given Tariq a bottle of whisky, although she knew he did not drink, and he had given her lily-of-the-valley cologne, which Mavis made clear she associated with old ladies. For Lou Tariq chose a book, Gramsci's *Prison Notebooks*, which went down with Mavis like a bucket of cold sick.

When they sat down for lunch things went from bad to worse. Louise sat at the head of the table and carved the turkey, a role she had taken on, ever since her father died. Her mother sat at the opposite end, issuing instructions to her younger daughter, and largely ignoring Verity and Tariq who sat one on each side of the table. Mavis had insisted Gladys wear her starched white uniform and that she provide silver service. As she stood to Tariq's right and served him vegetables from silver tureens, he spoke.

'What are your own family doing today, Gladys? When will

you see them next?'

'I am off for new year,' she replied, shooting Verity a frown.

Verity thought about Gladys returning to her quarters, located at a suitably servile distance at the bottom of her mother's garden, and spending the rest of Christmas alone. She was as mortified as Tariq but also angry at his implied criticism of her mother.

Mavis had bristled, and when Gladys returned to the kitchen, she glared at Tariq and invited him to keep his unsolicited opinions to himself. Tariq polished off his food with lightning speed, dabbed a starched napkin over tight lips and excused himself.

'Apologies Mrs Saunders, but I have to leave. I promised to do an afternoon shift at the hospital so my colleagues who celebrate Christmas can spend some time with their families.'

Verity had followed him to the car. 'That's rude and it's the first I've heard of you having to do a shift.'

'I think your mother was pretty rude too, Verity, and it's my choice to cover a shift. You may as well stay here because I won't be back at the apartment tonight. My mother has arranged for us to visit family friends, the Motalas, and their daughter Amira.'

'Why don't you include me in your family events like I do?'

'Precisely to protect you from awkward encounters like the one I have just endured.'

*   *   *

There was that name, Amira. At the time she had failed to imbue it with any significance. Had he been alone with her that night, just using his mother as an excuse? Verity thought about all the times when she had jealously imagined Tariq eating chicken biriyani with his mother, excluding her while they chewed over family gossip together, when the reality was so much worse. All those times when he supposedly retreated to his mother's place, or when he said he had to undertake an underground mission, had he really been wooing Amira?

Verity had always given Tariq the benefit of the doubt, always found reasons to forgive him, but this thing with Amira put a different complexion on things. Whatever explanation he came up with, she wasn't sure she could trust him again, and where did that leave her, pregnant with his child and in prison? When she thought of his love and excitement over their baby a fondness enveloped her. She wished she could hold onto the feeling, but the man on the tape kept reinserting himself into her troubled mind, and within seconds the feeling was obliterated.

10

As the summer progressed and the nights remained hot and humid, Verity struggled to sleep, falling in and out of consciousness through ever more fevered dreams. One night she was woken by a torch being shone directly in her face. Behind the beam she could make out a circle of shadowy figures in the cell, some still filing in. She crouched in her bed, shielded her eyes and pressed her back into the corner of the wall. Through parted fingers she saw a man drop his trousers, his erection bobbing as he played to an audience that began to stamp and cheer.

'Don't think your lily-white skin can protect you now, you cunt. You can shout if you want but nobody knows we're here,' someone said.

Her pyjama bottoms were yanked down, and she felt hands roughly spreading her legs. An arm across her throat garrotted her objections. Heaving his keg-like body on top of her a man pounded with relish, for enjoyment was not a word for this thing he was doing, this bravura exhibition performed for the benefit of a jeering pack of animals.

'You have a long wait, you guys, I can go like a train,' the man boasted to shouts of 'my turn' and 'me next'.

'Are you a cunt?' He growled at Verity. 'Say it you bitch. Say I'm a cunt, say I'm a commie cunt.'

The guttural chorus shifted to a chant of 'cunt, cunt, cunt', as the man pounded and pounded, breathing fumes of cheap brandy in her face. In a hoarse voice, Verity whispered that she was a cunt, and all the while the metal bedframe jacked against the wall.

A banging on the courtyard door gave them cause to quieten down. A man's voice shouted out, 'what the hell's going on in there?'

The flashlight swung away from her face and in its beam Verity recognised the black onyx ring that confirmed the identity of her assailant as he stood to shake himself off.

'Kom mense,' one of them said as they began trooping out of the cell door. 'Probably for the best. Better not to dip it in where a coolie has been.'

*   *   *

Verity could not shake off the presence of Kobus Swart. He stayed with her as pain. In her groin, the small of her back, the raw graze on her twisted shoulder, the crick in her neck. He lingered in the cramps in her stomach. Who were these men who thought they had the right to her body? How could Swart think he could suck up to his seniors by day, and bully by night, emptying his disgusting spunk into her? She craved the oblivion of sleep but couldn't face the sullied bed. She wrapped a sheet around herself and lay on the floor. She was sore and she was spent.

When she woke Verity's only thought was to wash away Swart's filthy deed. She tried to lift herself up but found she could not move. Her body was a throbbing bruise. She felt for the sheet beneath her. It was wet. She looked down and saw it was soaked with blood. Slowly she pushed herself into a sitting position and edged herself towards the wall. The movement produced another agonising gush. She looked between her legs and a silent scream pulsed through her like a person wrestling an enormous sorrow to the ground.

She could fit the foetus in the palm of her hand. He was tiny but perfectly formed. She nestled her son in her T-shirt, refusing to believe he was dead. She and Tariq had never discussed what they might call their baby, but she wanted to honour her little boy with a name. Tariq had said if it was a girl, she would be a little warrior like her mother. Limp as a flannel, Verity did not feel like a warrior but this little soul in her arms had fought just like one. Before even taking a breath, he had had to fight for life against Kobus Swart's brutal act. She remembered that Owen meant little warrior in Hebrew. There was probably a Muslim equivalent, but Tariq was not here to tell her what that was. Her child would be called Owen.

For hours she cradled him with a mother's delicacy that dared not pause for breath. She was insensible to the wide eyes of the young boys who delivered her uneaten breakfast and lunch. She was no longer eating for two. Sometime near dusk the sound of a metallic noise preceded the opening of the courtyard gate. Determined to expose her baby son to no more ugliness, and to protect him from any more of this inhumane world, she prised herself up. Unable to conceive of any other option, she placed her baby gently in the pan, and flushed.

Storming around like a fly shut in a closed room, Verity banged herself against the walls of the cell. She was barely aware of what she was doing, uttering, grunting, snarling, making noises she did not recognise. A great shuddering wave washed through her making her spine convulse. She collapsed onto the floor where she stayed while the light faded, her insides still shaking where her anger resided.

Her eyes settled on the untouched meal trays and the tin mugs without their handles. An idea took root. They could keep their mug handles. She took off her bra and with fevered excitement gnawed at the sweaty cotton until she produced a hole in the fabric large enough to pull out the smiling underwire from beneath the cup. She gnawed some more to remove the little globule designed to stop the wire's sharpness from digging into bosomy flesh. It came off in her teeth along with the metallic taste of blood. Tariq was gone, little Owen was no more, soon she too would be gone. She had been in this prison so long, she no longer existed for others. Her absence would barely be noticed.

*   *   *

Verity felt her body half held, half dragged by two uniformed officers, one at each elbow. Lines of sweat ran from her crown to her neck, and on down her spine. She tried walking straight so as not to draw attention to herself but crumpled in their hold. They veered along corridors that were new to her. The stares of prison staff, standing in corners around buckets and mops, followed her. These guards and cleaners were the real inhabitants of this underworld, she thought, spending year after year on the prison's margins, scraping along at the bottom of the pile. No wonder they had that aimless look in their eyes, devoid of curiosity. Are they horrified by what they see in here, or do they just assume this is how life is? In a shadowy corner she thought she saw Jan Niemand.

In an elevator she caught a glimpse of herself in a mirror for the first time in months. She was barely recognisable to herself, freckles faded, skin taut, her brow studded with sweat, and her eyes fixed in a five-mile stare. In a basement car park Verity was folded into the back of a car, someone seated at her side.

They drove into an evening where giant throngs of flying ants clustered around the streetlights. She had read somewhere that these airborne termites engaged in one seasonal orgiastic extravaganza before the females turned to reproduction and the males crawled off to die. Like Tariq, she thought, dimly conscious that he was still out there somewhere believing he'd fathered a growing child, unaware that she had failed to keep her side of the bargain.

They pulled into a car park and when the interior light of the police car came on, flying ants swarmed towards it. Hard shells banged against the windows, their translucent under-sides splattering against the glass. Verity was lifted into a wheelchair and pushed into a building, down corridors with glaring lights above and linoleum beneath. The porter punched numbers into a unit on a locked ward door. The corridor had no windows, just doorways. Through one that was open she saw a woman shuffling towards her, her eyes vacant, a nurse holding her arm. From prison to hospital, another world with no weather, no clocks, and time standing still. Even the nurse's watch hung upside down.

Verity was only vaguely aware of the spectral figures who drifted in and out of her sleep. Mostly ethereal, some tangible, like the hand that gripped her wrist from time to time. Hallucinatory voices wished her well, others spoke words of madness. Tariq was among them weaving threads of revolutionary rhetoric. I thought you were dead, she told him. Her father floated in, sitting on the platform of a pick-up truck, the breeze lifting his fine hair from his scalp as he smoked a cigarette. The ash burned and the lit end got ever closer to his fingers. 'Daddy!' she cried out, trying to warn him. Her arm reached out to touch him, but he was not at its end, just her outstretched fingers recoiling in a fist from the iron side of her hospital bed.

'Where am I?' Verity asked the person at the end of a cool hand on her forehead.

'In hospital, in the psychiatric ward. Where have *you* been more like? That was some choice language you were using, Verity. Welcome back to the real world.'

Verity squinted waiting for the voice to morph into human shape. The curtains of the room were drawn against the outside light. Kaleidoscopic images and inane babble emanated from cartoons on a TV mounted on the wall.

'It seems you've had a rough run of it, Verity,' said the nurse, 'but I think it's time you had a bath, for all our sakes.'

She helped Verity out of the bed, gathered up the sheets drenched with sweat, and dropped them in a canvas laundry bag.

'Gita,' the nurse turned to a policewoman sitting in a large wingback chair, 'if we leave the door ajar, do you think Miss Saunders can bathe alone?'

'Fine by me,' Gita replied, her eyes fixed on the cartoons.

The bathroom was only a few steps from the bed, but Verity's legs gave, and her hands shook when the nurse offered her a flannel.

'I've run you a bath dear. Have a nice long soak. You've more or less stopped bleeding down below, but you need to keep this arm out of the water. We don't want your bandages to get wet.

I'll come back in a while and help you wash your hair.'

Verity lowered herself into the tub, lay back gingerly, then slipped under the deep warm water, one arm raised in a salute of failure as she dimly recalled doing battle on her wrist with the underwire of her bra.

'Troublesome hair you have,' said the nurse returning with the shampoo, 'so thick and wavy.'

Apologetically, Verity told her about the lice.

'Oh, okay, let's leave it for the time being. I'll order a treatment. Just concentrate on re-joining us in the here and now. Things will get better, I promise.'

Verity sat on the edge of the bath and dried herself with a towel that felt too fluffy. She wanted her prison towel back, so worn and rough that it scraped her body like sandpaper.

She returned to the ward and saw that apart from the bed and the visitor's chair occupied by the policewoman, the only other furniture in the small private ward was a bedside table.

'I'm Gita,' said the policewoman. 'In case you hadn't realised, although you're in hospital you're still a prisoner, under twenty-four-hour armed guard. I'm here to stop you from topping yourself or your comrades from trying to jump you.'

'Chance would be a fine thing,' said Verity. 'Do you know how long I'll be here?'

'Don't know and couldn't tell you if I did. My instructions are not to talk to you at all. But it's boring sitting here all day and anyway, who is going to know if we have a conversation? So, if you want to talk it's fine. Just don't ask me any awkward questions, okay?'

'Okay,' Verity agreed. 'Can we try another TV channel, if that's not an awkward question?'

'The question's fine, the answer's no. We're only allowed the cartoon channel in case news, or a current affairs programme comes on. You're not supposed to know what's going on out there.'

'What is going on out there?'

'That's an awkward question,' she grinned.

The next day the nurse appeared with the lice treatment. She combed the lotion through Verity's matted hair with a fine-toothed comb, which gave Verity mild electric shocks, but the softness of her strokes brought a tightness to her throat, and Verity found herself welling up. Well defended against adversity when it came from the outside, it was the assault of kindness that knocked her off her guard.

'Let it go,' said the nurse. 'Better out than in.'

With that the tears gushed. Finally, the dam had broken and Verity was swept along with the flood.

Hospital, like prison, was characterised by stretches of monotony punctuated by periodic unwelcome interruptions. One of these was a regular visit from the state psychiatrist, who sat in the visitor's chair hunched over his notebook, peering at Verity from behind glasses that had quarried a permanent groove across the ridge of his nose. It was the only time Gita left the room and although Verity had braced herself for questions about her childhood, they were not forthcoming. He seemed entirely indifferent to her past or her future, his sole interest being in giving her lectures on the matter of personal responsibility.

'I know all about discrimination and injustice,' he said, 'but I take my cue from the United States of America.'

'Okay,' Verity said, unsure of where he might be going with this.

'On the east coast stands the Statue of Liberty, symbolising freedom. On the west coast you have Alcatraz, you know, the prison.'

'And so?' she asked, fixating on the hairs sprouting from

his nostrils.

'With freedom comes responsibility. Understand?' He stood up as if he had made himself perfectly clear. 'You seek freedom, Miss Saunders, but your actions have consequences. It's no good blaming your mother, the government, or Tariq and Imran. You are responsible for your own actions, and you are here because you're being held to account.'

Where in hell had he got hold of those names, Verity wanted to ask him, and from whom did he take his steer? As he was paid for his services by the apartheid state, there were no prizes for guessing. So much for freedom anyway, she thought. While Imran and Tariq were chasing their own respective liberty statues, she was the one stuck in Alcatraz.

Like prison, the nights were not much better than the days, and sometimes they were worse. Here she had no privacy at all, and the night officer was a different being from Gita. When they changed shift Verity would try and listen in to their handover in the corridor. She caught only the odd phrase, usually from Gita, like, 'she's been no trouble at all,' and 'she's actually quite sweet, friendly in fact'. Replies from the night duty policewoman were taciturn and rule-bound, and Verity never held a conversation with her, she did not even learn her name. The night officer only dropped her guard once, when her policeman boyfriend came to visit her in the ward. Verity could smell the state of emergency on him, the teargas, and the fear. She lay rigid in her bed pretending to be asleep, while they made out in the visitors' chair. As his hands roamed the policewoman's body she wondered if they had blood on them.

*   *   *

'So, you really had no idea I was coming?' said Louise as she perched a buttock on the edge of Verity's bed.

Verity shook her head and stared at her sister in amazement, as though an apparition had manifested in front of her. 'Louise, how long have I been in prison? How did you get in?'

'We were granted one visit, and this is it,' Louise said, breaking down. She quickly pulled herself together and wiped away her tears, but Verity could see this was not the first time her red-rimmed eyes had cried that day.

'It's been too long V. You've never been far from my mind. We tried to get permission to visit you in prison, but they refused. You know I would have come if they'd let me.'

'It's fine, Lou, I know how it is. I just can't believe it's really you.' Verity pushed herself up straighter in the bed and reached out to hug her sister.

'Come on, don't you start too. We've only got a short time and we don't want to waste it crying. There's so much to catch up on.'

Gita, who was reclining in the visitor's chair paging through a fashion magazine, glanced up. 'No contact, no politics.'

Louise slowly withdrew from her sisters embrace.

'We heard what happened. Are you ok V?'

Verity tugged at the cuff of her hospital gown to cover her bandage and sighed. 'Yes, I'm doing alright. They have a psychiatrist who comes to talk to me about responsibility and accountability and gives me these little white pills, but I'm fine, I'm on the mend, Lou. How's mum doing?'

'It's been tough on her V, there's no getting away from it, and you know what she's like. She lashes out and I know she can say hurtful things, but she's worried sick about you.'

'Why didn't she come and visit then?' Verity's jaw was set.

'Don't be like that, V. Honestly, she would have come with me, but they would only allow one of us. Try and see it from her side. She can't bring herself to think what you've been through, let alone see you in this state. A couple of people tried to drum her out of the tennis club, can you believe it? They said anyone whose daughter fraternised with terrorists was not welcome. But you wouldn't believe the dressing down she gave them. You should have heard her, Verity, saying you were not a terrorist and in fact it was them who were the delinquents. Please tell me you didn't do anything wrong, V, that you weren't really linked to terrorism?'

'I'm not going to dignify that with an answer,' Verity said stiffly.

'Good,' said Gita, 'because I'm still here and I must remind you again Louise Saunders, no politics talk. You were given permission to visit, to talk about family and to bring some flowers but the rules are strict, no talk about what's going on in the country and definitely no politics.'

'Of course, I'm so sorry,' Louise said turning back to Verity, 'and I nearly forgot to give you the flowers.' She reached down to the floor and held up a bundle of red and yellow gladioli, wrapped in paper. 'I thought these would help brighten up your room for a while.' As she passed them over to Verity, she turned her back on Gita and mouthed the words, 'read the newspaper inside, it's from Yasmin.'

Verity took hold of the flowers and from the bright pink crepe paper that was scrunched around the stems she picked out a folded sheet of newsprint and slipped it beneath her gown.

'I'm sorry you two, but time is nearly up, so begin to say your goodbyes,' said Gita without taking her eyes from the cartoon playing on the TV.

The two sisters looked at each other saying nothing, both

fighting back the tears they did not want the other to see. Louise took Verity's clenched fists in her own and prised open her fingers, weaving them between hers to form a cradle, just as they had done when they were children. 'You'll be out of here soon, V, I'm sure of it.'

Verity held on to her sister's hand, but Gita called time. Reluctantly Louise lifted herself from the edge of the bed and backed away, not breaking eye contact with Verity until she rounded the ward door. Then she quickly put her head back around and blew her a kiss. 'Everything's going to be fine. Oh, I forgot to mention, I defrosted your fridge.'

'Your sister's nice. Good to have a visit hey,' said Gita, 'There's a vase in your bedside cupboard if you want to put the flowers in water.'

Verity swung her legs from the bed, fetched the vase and took the flowers into the bathroom. She filled the vase with water and placed it on the toilet seat, then tore off the crepe paper and arranged the flowers. Putting her head round the half-open door she saw that Gita was still absorbed in her magazine. Delicately she unfolded the half sheet of newsprint and a headline immediately caught her eye, *Bombing at Beachfront Bar*. The short article reported that a car bomb had gone off outside a beachfront bar in Durban, which was a well-known watering hole frequented by the security police. It had killed three people and injured more. Verity's knees folded and she sat down heavily on the side of the bath, wondering if the culprit had been anyone she knew. Imran had form having blown up an electricity pylon in the past. There was no doubt that Tariq was in his thrall, but his was a political cell dealing with communications, not a military unit.

Verity turned over the sheet of newspaper and saw on the other side a small pencil cross next to the article Yasmin had meant her to read.

Senior ANC Terrorist Captured. Imran Malik, a senior member of the ANC leadership is in Pretoria Central Prison awaiting trial for treason. This known terrorist who served ten years on Robben Island was captured at an ANC safe house in Swaziland. Another man was killed in the scuffle. A spokesman for National Intelligence said that they were still looking for another person of interest, Dr Tariq Randeree, who is thought to have left the country at the same time as Malik, and his whereabouts are currently unknown.

As she got to the last line an involuntary gasp escaped Verity's lips as relief washed the tension from her body. If they were still looking for Tariq, then he had not been the man killed at the safe house.

'Verity, are you okay in there?'

'Sorry, Gita. I've got an upset stomach. It must be the stress of seeing my sister. I'll be out in a minute. I'm cramping.'

'I don't need the details.'

Verity turned on the taps, tore up the newsprint and flushed it down the toilet.

*   *   *

After four more days in the hospital the state psychiatrist visited again and informed Verity that she would be returned to prison that day. He wrote out a prescription for more pills, called in a nurse and told her to ensure the pharmacy had it ready within the hour.

'What are those for?' Verity asked.

'Depression and anxiety. We can't risk anymore histrionics, can we?'

In her newly washed prison tracksuit, Verity was escorted by Gita to the hospital dispensary where she was told to take a seat and wait. She vowed she would not take any more of the noxious pills that rendered her blank and inert, knowing that when she got back to her cell the warders would not have the patience to stand over her like the nurses did here, making sure she swallowed.

Once the pills had been dispensed, a uniformed policeman arrived and led her out to an unmarked van. He and Gita exchanged signatures on some paperwork and as she helped Verity into the back of the vehicle, Gita said, 'I hope things work out for you, Verity.'

It was hot and dirty in the back of the van, and by the time the journey was over, Verity's freshly laundered tracksuit was looking more like its old filthy version of itself. The corridors of the prison were empty, and she was deposited back in her old cell without a word being spoken.

Solitude held a strange comfort. It was a relief not to have an officer sitting right next to her all day and all night, a gun at arm's length from her head. Yet as summer days gave way to the cooler dry season, Verity's spirit flagged. She spent her days lying about in her tracksuit with the coarse grey blanket around her shoulders. She could no longer stand the smell of carbolic soap and stopped washing both herself and her clothes. Any sense of who she was had been squeezed out of her. Hope was now a wayward companion.

PART 2

PART 9

12

The suite at the Piazza Apartment Hotel had barely changed in thirty years. With its matching bottle-green and liver-pink curtains and bedcover, and its dark wood furniture, the place was designed not to show the dirt. Images buried for decades pressed down on Verity now. She thought about the time she had smuggled Tariq into a room just like this. She pictured him lying back on the floral counterpane, the feather of hairs running down his sternum, his hands locked behind his neck. Despite once being at its beating heart, for years now Tariq had been nothing more than a ghostly presence in her life, but Sergio's death had rendered him alive again. She supposed one loss could resurrect another, and maybe this visit was just a distraction from her widow's grief.

From the moment Verity had boarded the overnight flight from Heathrow she'd felt disoriented. At one level it was a flight like any other; instructions to put tray tables back, warnings about things moving in overhead lockers, the handing out of scratchy blankets and bendy little toothbrushes designed for single use. At another level though, it was momentous. During the night the plane had dropped sharply in a pocket of turbulence, sending every person on board into prayer to their various deities. She had reached for Sergio's hand, a pathetic, futile reflex that had sent the stone of grief lodged in her stomach travelling upwards towards her throat. She touched the terracotta bead necklace, his last gift to her, and spoke to him in her head. If you could see me now Sergio Vargas, what would you say?

When they began their final descent her stomach had lurched again - this time mirroring the dread she used to feel when returning from doing overseas courier jobs for the ANC - and she had to remind herself that these were new times. Through the window she watched the barren plains of ochre earth pockmarked by black rocks, give way to Johannesburg's familiar city limits. Low-income settlements with their own rough edges of makeshift shacks, still bled into suburbs with wider roads, bigger houses, and greener plots. Little blue rectangles and kidney shapes signalled the splashy, pool-based entertainment of the middle-classes, now no longer the confine of white South Africans alone.

She remembered the blast of hot dry air that had hit her when she descended the aircraft steps in the past, and how she had to steady herself by grabbing onto aluminium railings almost too hot to hold. This time exiting passengers were steered from the plane through a concertina tunnel that fed directly into an air-conditioned terminal. Verity headed for the foreign visitors' queue at passport control, which moved forward remarkably efficiently, and retrieved her case from the baggage carousel. In the hustle and bustle of the Arrivals Terminal she noted with a little stir of satisfaction, that black people were not only there as porters and baggage handlers but predominated among the passengers too.

At the car hire desk the man in front of her began hustling for an upgrade.

'I asked for a black BMW!'

The desk clerk, whose name badge read Ntombi Dlamini, glanced over at Verity apologetically, then explained to the man that their stock was limited, because most people preferred white cars as they deflect the heat.

'That's nonsense! With aircon it doesn't matter what colour the car is.'

'I know Mr Dube, Sir, but I don't purchase the cars.'

He drummed his fingers on the counter, shaking his head, the beaded braids at the end of his cornrows swinging across the nape of his neck. In the end he settled for a discount on a white BMW and sauntered off spinning his suitcase, clearly a winner.

'Eish, thanks for waiting,' the clerk said flashing Verity a smile and making a tsk sound with her tongue against her teeth. 'These Black Diamonds give me grief.'

'Black Diamonds?'

'The new rich. He's a Born Free like me but he thinks he's it, wants to flash the cash.' She gave a deep laugh.

'Born Free?'

'Born after apartheid. Can I have your passport and driving licence? Okay, I see you're a Britisher, is it your first time here? Welcome to South Africa.'

'I was here a long time ago,' Verity said, feeling an unwarranted sense of shame.

'If you want to see how it was, you can go to the Apartheid Museum. It's near Soweto. Or you can talk to my parents,' Ntombi said with another throaty laugh. 'They go on about the bad old days all the time, telling me I don't know how lucky I am!'

By the time Verity made it to her hotel suite, she was tired and hungry. Not wanting to wait for room service she downed a bottle of water, ate all the complementary biscuits, pulled on her pyjamas and climbed into bed. Lying back, she gave into an exhaustion born of long-haul travel, packing up her apartment, handing over to her cover at work and winding down the rest of her life. She slept through until dawn.

It was her recurring dream that woke her. It had disappeared when Sergio had danced her out of the shadows, but it had returned with his death. Once again her old ghosts had made their reappearance and she seemed unable to keep them at bay. The sepia sequence of undulating khaki that was her cell, and the malodourous figure of Kobus Swart slowly faded as daylight made itself known through a gap in the sombre curtains. Verity hauled the dark green and pink bedcover over her exposed limbs and waited for her heart rate to return to normal.

Burying her face in the pillow Verity berated Sergio for dying. She thought she had lost the capacity for rage. Irritation, yes, annoyance, of course. It was not unknown for her to shout 'fuckwit!' at an irresponsible driver, but this anger was fresh. She swilled it around in her head, trying it on for size, pummelling her pillows back into shape, as if trying to put some order into the unruly fabric of her life, asking herself why she had returned to the country that had brought her to her knees.

She calmed herself and made the bed, smoothing the creases in the counterpane and noticing with faint disapproval that the sombre floral pattern did not line up properly at the seams. She was here now, and for better or for worse there was no going back. I have inverted the hourglass of my life, she sighed, and the sand has already started running back towards my past. If I am unable to discover what happened to Tariq, then at least I might find out why they did what they did to me.

Verity made herself a cup of tea and turned on the TV, which hummed to life with a message welcoming her to Johannesburg and wishing her an enjoyable stay in the 'City of Gold'. As she scrolled though a list of the hotel services her mobile beeped with a text message alert.

Thanks for sending me your South African cell phone number. I have updates. It would be good to speak. Even better we could meet in person. Donny van Rooyen.

Verity had been put in touch with van Rooyen by a British journalist, a friend of Sergio's called Will Parker. He had told her van Rooyen was helpful to him when he had been a foreign correspondent in Johannesburg during the last years of apartheid and that despite some dubious connections, he was generally considered to be a good egg across the political spectrum, and someone who might be well equipped to help her track down Tariq.

She responded to van Rooyen's message, suggesting he join her at the Piazza for happy hour, in the Lord Dunkeld Snug, later in the week, then lifted her laptop from her hand luggage to skim over her previous correspondence with him. She had emailed him to tell him about her visit and had enquired as to whether he could help her track down certain people she wished to interview for her research into the Truth and Reconciliation Commission. She had told this half-truth because her instinct was not to trust him. He had replied that any friend of Will Parker's was a friend of his and that he looked forward to meeting her when she arrived in South Africa.

Verity closed down the laptop, sat back down on the bed and tried to dispel her fears about the journey she was about to embark upon.

13

It was in a dim bar in Kilburn on a wintry London afternoon that Verity had met up with Will Parker. He wore a Viyella shirt and tweed jacket that had seen better days, but his tan brogues were polished to a military shine.

'Thanks for meeting me, Will, and thanks for coming to Sergio's memorial,' Verity had said as she slid over his pint of ale and sat down at the table.

'Not a bit of it. It was quite a turn out.'

'It was, and important because his funeral in Colombia was such a small family affair. I wanted his memorial to be a celebration of the hugely public man he was.' Verity wiped the rim of the cloudy pub glass with a tissue and poured her sparkling water.

'Well, you certainly did my old pal proud, Verity Vargas.'

'I hope so. I choreographed the whole event down to the last detail, but when it came to it, the day just passed in a blur as I watched Sergio's life pass before my eyes.'

'And too short a life it was. The world has lost a damn good journalist. You know what I loved so much about him? He always knew what side he was on. That YouTube clip you found showed exactly that. He really told those international donors where to get off.'

'Thank you for your money,' Verity had said, citing Sergio's speech. 'When you have money, people smile and nod at your ideas, seat you at the best table at gala dinners. That does not give you the right to tell people what to do. For centuries, the people of the Amazon have protected their land and waters. Why do you think you know better than them now? You don't give money to a brain surgeon then tell him how to perform his surgery. Listen to these people and their wisdom so you don't destroy their lives and our shared planet.'

'You've got it off pat there, girl. Stirring stuff. Sergio was the real deal, not like the modern youngsters. They do their time as cubs on local rags, but don't really learn to investigate. Today's modus operandi is to get everything off the inter-web. Not good enough, I say. If you want to know France, you have to go there and smell the Gauloises. Get my drift?' Parker waved his empty pipe to make his point.

Verity had nodded and watched as he returned the pipe to a jacket pocket shot through with tiny shrapnel-like punctures, suggesting he sometimes stowed it away still glowing.

'I don't blame them, though,' Parker continued, 'budgets these days don't stretch to the deep hanging out we used to do. Think about the insights Sergio got from allowing himself to be kidnapped by the FARC, and the stuff he wrote afterwards was fantastic. I think his reporting contributed to the recent peace talks in Colombia.'

'I do too,' said Verity as she thought back to how she had stood at Sergio's grave side in Bogotá, asking herself, is this is what it comes to, covering your soaring spirit in suffocating mud?'

'He certainly lived life to the full, our Sergio. What was that song the memorial ended with? It had everybody dancing out of the door.'

'Marc Anthony, *Vivir mi Vida*' Verity said, 'live my life.' As she had said the words she smiled at the image of people dancing to it, how they had opened their memorial booklets and waved them in the air like a flock of birds, a swooping murmuration of warmth and love. She had imagined then Sergio soaring skywards, for his element was air not earth.

'Anyway, we're here to talk about my trip to South Africa,' she said, pulling herself back to the moment. 'You were based in Johannesburg for a long time, Will. You must have known a lot of people I could talk to.'

'Yep, people in government, the movement, business, the lot – the good, the bad and the ugly.' Parker wiped foam from his upper lip with a well-practiced tongue. 'But Verity, are you sure it's a good idea? Things there have changed a lot. How long since you were back?'

'Over thirty years.'

'You never returned? Why?'

'I had a traumatic time. The man I was in love with disappeared off the face of the earth. Another man I was involved with politically was abducted and jailed. Things were very difficult with my family. So, I left and tried to build a new life in London. Just when that began to feel impossible, I met Serge and at that point I decided to put the whole sorry experience behind me and live my life, *Vivir mi Vida*.'

'Until now?'

'Until now.'

'And you think it's a good idea to open old wounds on top of these new ones?'

'They're already open, Will, they opened with Serge's death.'

'I don't want to come across as negative, Verity, but people have moved on. Do you really think they'll appreciate you pitching up and probing into memories they'd rather leave undisturbed?'

'Who knows? If people won't talk to me, then at least I can check out the South African archives.'

'You'll be lucky. They're in a parlous state.' He took his pipe back out from his pocket and sucked on it thoughtfully. 'I suspect the Truth and Reconciliation Commission records are the best you've got. I presume you've looked at those?'

'Yes, I went through all the TRC transcripts in the British Library. What about police and government papers, like National Intelligence records?'

'Are you serious? Haven't you heard of the Bonfire of the Vanities?' Parker snorted.

'The Tom Wolfe book?' Verity laughed.

'No, it was what happened when negotiations to form a government of national unity were taking place. The ANC asked that the proceedings listen to a 1988 tape of a conversation held between President, P.W. Botha, and Nelson Mandela while he was in prison, but it wasn't there. The ANC went ballistic, demanded an immediate stop to the destruction of state records, but it was too late, pfffft.' Will made an upward gesture with both his hands, his fingers splaying out. 'There was a mass destruction of all security police records. In the space of six months over forty metric tonnes of evidence - truckloads of paper files, recording tapes, computer disks, microfilm, the lot, all incinerated, shredded or wiped, just a year before the first democratic elections.'

'That's terrible,' Verity said, although she felt emotionally ambivalent thinking back to the recordings the Tapeworm had played back to her.

'Yep, it was, but after that initial protest, the outrage fizzled out.'

'Why?'

'For some people it came as a gift. To have the historical record eradicated meant their past could remain in the past. All the traitors and turncoats on both sides escaped unscathed, some getting government jobs, others making a fortune in business. The less fortunate or smart, of course, continued to skulk around in the margins forever.'

'There's something else I wanted to ask you about,' she said. 'I read about something called Operation Phezulu. Do you know anything about it?'

'Phezulu,' Parker said, taking a deep draught of his ale. 'It was something dreamed up by a faction of the ANC leadership in the mid-80s, mostly exiles who were also in the South African Communist Party. Quite an impressive operation, actually.'

'Why impressive?'

'At that time the apartheid intelligence service was at the top of its game. Their spies had infiltrated all levels of the ANC, but especially Umkhonto weSizwe, the armed struggle chappies. Those MK cadres began falling like flies, and the level of trust within the movement was at a very low ebb. The exiled leadership was worried it was out of touch with the mood inside country, and they were right to be worried. The revolution was happening without them. A couple of them were smuggled back into the country, but the real breakthrough was when Operation Phezulu set up this communications network that did away with reliance on old methods like dead letter boxes, and couriers. Don't ask me about the technology but Phezulu was sophisticated for the time, some kind of precursor to the internet.'

All this had gelled with Verity. The task of their cell had been communications, and Tariq was forever buried in his computer which he always secreted away after use, and Imran must have been one of those smuggled operatives.

'If it was so closed and effective, how was it discovered?' she asked.

'Completely by chance after MK muscled in on the action. A former comrade who was turned and spied for apartheid –'

'An askari?'

'Yep, that's what I believe they called them, anyhow this askari was in Johannesburg minding his own business when he recognised an ANC soldier he knew from when he was in exile. He reported the fellow to his bosses, and the chap was arrested. Unfortunately for Phezulu, he was carrying the system's coding disks and boom! Overnight the whole operation was busted.'

'How come MK got involved?'

'They came in late when the ANC began preparing for negotiations. Some in the ANC thought the apartheid government would never willingly hand over power and set up a Plan B, which was armed insurrection. They took over Phezulu networks to arrange the movement of military people and equipment into the country, without being detected.'

'Where did the money come from?'

'Good question. I always follow the money. As far as I understand things, the GDR was the main international funder.'

'Do you have any East German contacts I could speak to?'

'You must be joking! In any event, these days it's as hard to find anyone admitting they worked for the Stasi as it is to find those who admit to supporting apartheid.'

'And people in South Africa?'

'I've been thinking about that. You could do worse than Donny van Rooyen. I'm not sure he's your type though. He used to work for the security police, but good people seemed to rate his networks and discretion. He's retired, I think, but still fancies himself as a bit of a sleuth.' Parker rummaged through his pockets and pulled out a scrap of paper and a fountain pen. 'Here's his email address, drop him a line and say Will Parker vouches for you.'

'Thank you, Will...and one last thing, do you know if Imran Malik was involved in Phezulu?'

'Quite likely. He was a big fish in the external mission and a communist. So, you knew him?' Over the rim of his pint glass Parker gave Verity a long, hard look. 'Did you see he's just been made Minister of Education? He'll be in London next month to attend the World Education Forum.'

'Thanks for the tip off. I'll make sure I bump into him,' said Verity, perking up at this news. 'What about Tariq Randeree, was he part of it?'

'No idea, did you know him too?'

'I worked with him back in the day, he got me into the movement. I used to do some foreign courier runs for them before...well...before things changed. I'm just trying to find out what happened to him.'

Parker lifted his empty glass and put it down again. 'It's not a name I'm familiar with, sorry I can't help you there. Well, I guess all I can say is good luck, but are you sure you're ready for this, Verity?'

Verity slowly nodded, trying to dispel any remaining doubts she may have harboured about her decision to return.

14

Verity had not seen her sister since leaving Durban all those years ago. As she drove towards her house she tried to breathe away the knot of anxiety in her stomach and focus on her surroundings instead. Johannesburg was much as she remembered it; railway lines, highways, flyovers, junctions, water towers, electricity sub-stations, all deliberately located to keep white suburbs and black townships apart. Shacks and informal settlements were now squeezed in between them but the material legacies of how society had once been separately planned still persisted.

Following Louise's directions, Verity turned off the highway onto tree lined streets where houses skulked behind high walls topped with razor wire. When she saw the sign for Hlanganani Lifestyle Estate she turned in and pulled up at the gatehouse. A guard consulted his clipboard, phoned the house, then raised the boom. Verity drove slowly, following the guard's directions, and as she approached the house she saw Louise and Hanneli were waiting for her at the front door. Above them was a sign on the lintel with the words Oos Wes Tuis Bes. As Verity pulled up and got out of the car, Louise came bounding down the steps, her long tanned legs accentuated by the high line of her shorts.

'Let me take a good look at you. Eish, I'd forgotten what a short arse you are,' Louise said, giving Verity a squeeze.

'Howzit, Verity!' said Hanneli, pulling the sisters into an embrace. 'We meet at last, in the flesh. I'm so sorry about Sergio, sweetie.'

She released them from the group hug and they stood there in a circle, holding hands, just staring at each other. The moment of connection was interrupted as a flurry of dogs rushed down the steps and bounded around them.

'You have to meet the dogs as well. This is Simba,' said Hanneli, giving an enormous Ridgeback a pat, 'and this is Cheeky Boy. He's an Africanis, now a recognised African breed. So, you're no longer a brak my lovely boy,' she said, rubbing him behind his ears.'

'And this is my baby,' said Louise, as she scooped up a fluffy, wriggling creature that lavished her face with licks. 'Come on in and see the house.'

Verity followed them through the front door and into a large open plan living room. The dogs fussed around her feet, their claws clicking on the tiled floor.

'Paws on the floor!' commanded Louise, and the dogs obediently sat, tongues lolling. 'So welcome to our humble abode V, hope you like it? Most of the stylish furniture comes from Hanneli's ouma, antiques from when the family sold their farm. Just look at that yellowwood dresser, it's beautiful, hey?'

Verity stood trying to take it all in. The whole vibe of the room was African and Africana, in a gorgeously mixed-up way. A low carved stinkwood coffee table was strewn with magazines;

Huisgenoot, The Indigenous Gardener, and *LGBT Africa,* and next to a wood burner was a staggered trio of Zulu dolls in beaded felt, their elongated necks encircled by metal chokers.

'Lou brought those with her from Durban,' said Hanneli, as she followed Verity's gaze. 'And it was her idea to cover all of the cushions in shweshwe. Mave, I mean your mother, brought the other Zulu beadwork things with her when she came to stay.'

'It's a beautiful place you have,' said Verity. The mention of her mother brought back ambivalent memories of Mavis and a familiar twinge of guilt. 'I owe you a lot Hanni. Thank you so much for looking after her and for being there for Lou.'

'It was nothing, and your sister has been a rock for us all,' said Hanni as she gave Louise a squeeze.

'Right then, enough of all this soppiness, come while I check on the braai, V. Hanni needs to do the salad. Wait till you taste it, the best salad you'll eat in your life.'

'The flame trees along your street are gorgeous,' said Verity as they moved out into the garden. 'They must be amazing in flower.'

'Ja, but Flamboyant trees are alien.' Lou tucked some stray hairs behind her ears and poked the coals on the barbeque. 'Our garden is entirely indigenous.'

'Really? I can't even see a bougainvillea,' Verity said, looking around. 'You used to love those.'

'Alien,' Louise insisted.

Verity looked at the acacia trees along the boundary of the garden and thought, indigenous but thorny, like Lou, who always took what she said as implicit criticism. She saw the telltale tuck appear at the corner of her sister's mouth that signalled upset. The last time she had seen it was when Lou had collected her on her release from prison.

*   *   *

'Who's here to collect Verity Saunders? She needs signing for,' the duty sergeant had barked out across the varnished counter. Lou had risen from where she was sitting and accepted the chewed ballpoint he had offered her. Once the paperwork had been signed, and Verity was reunited with her confiscated watch, they left the prison waiting room in silence. Outside Verity shrugged off Lou's attempt at a hug as she blinked against the shimmering macadam and the sun-bleached façade of the prison. She wanted to get far away from its brutal presence and as quickly as possible. 'Come on. Let's go,' she'd said, only realising later how hostile and cold she must have seemed.

Lou had simply shrugged, handed her a pair of sunglasses, and opened the car door, that stoic tuck displayed at the corner of her mouth. 'Come on you,' she said, cupping Verity's face in her large hands. 'Let's get you home.'

'Can we drive past the beach? I've been dying to feel sand and water on my feet.'

'Okay, a quick stop. Mave is waiting for us.'

The sand was scorching as Verity sprinted down to the shoreline. She suddenly felt dizzy, unaccustomed to moving at speed, or to the large expanse of space after the confines of her cell. She steadied herself as the ripples of tail-end waves washed around her ankles, only looking up when Louise's red painted toes appeared alongside her own, too-long, yellowed nails.

'V, I need to get something off my chest. I'm sorry to spring this on you so soon...'

'What?'

'I took the decision while you...I didn't know what to do... we didn't renew the lease on your apartment. I couldn't afford to keep up with the rent, and Mave was never going to help out. With no contribution coming from Tariq...' Louise tailed off, sounding distraught. 'I brought your stuff home. At least you've got a roof over your head.'

'With Mum?' Verity looked incredulous. 'What about Tariq's things?'

'To be honest, there wasn't much. I left a box with the letting agent for Yasmin to collect.'

Verity stepped further into the shallows, staring out at the container vessels lining the horizon. It was true, she thought with an ache. He had paid the lion's share of the rent, but he never really left his mother's house. A twist of salt air caught in her throat and, unable to speak, she had tried to arrange her face in the shape of gratitude.

When they pulled up to the house, Mavis Saunders was waiting on the front steps and rushed towards Verity, anxiously kissing her on both cheeks, before standing back to survey her.

'My dear girl! You're so pale, your skin is grey,' she said, looking quite gaunt herself.

'I expect so. I've been inside for a long time. Indoors, I mean.'

'Well, both, don't you think?' said Louise, eliciting from Verity the first flash of a grin. 'Come, V, let me show you what I've done with your things.'

Under the windowsill in her childhood bedroom stood the piles of boxes from her apartment that Louise had packed up. Along the top of the chest of drawers Verity noticed that her old dolls were lined up, their arms raised, as if reaching for the ceiling.

'Why have all the dolls got their arms up?'

Mavis, who had followed them in said coyly, 'it was me, they're saying welcome home.'

'I think that's a sweet thing to do, don't you?' Louise said.

'Now why don't you get yourself settled in, you must be overwhelmed. We'll get supper ready while you have a lie down.'

'Thank you, it's a nice touch,' said Verity.

When their mother had left the room Louise whispered, 'please think of something reassuring to tell Mave later, I mean, if you can think of anything. She's been worried sick about you, V.'

Verity nodded and sighed the shuddery breath of a small child. Alone she stretched out on the single bed and picked at the old peach-coloured candlewick spread, adding new worries to a bald patch, the legacy of infant anxieties. Fighting back tears, she scraped the filaments of cotton into a fluff ball, dropped it in the wastepaper basket and tried to get some sleep before having to try and reassure her mother.

That evening they had eaten supper off trays on their laps and Mavis was discretion itself. Verity guessed Lou must have had a word. They talked easily about things that had happened while Verity was away, '*away*' being the euphemism they seemed to have adopted to refer to her time in prison. They discussed things like who won the women's singles and doubles matches at the tennis club tournament, and old school friends who had got married or given birth. After a while, Louise had said she had things to do and that she would leave them to catch up.

'I couldn't sleep while you were away,' Mavis said when they were alone, but the tick of accusation so often in her voice had been absent.

'I'm sorry,' Verity replied. 'Do you want a whisky?' She got up and poured her mother her usual double tot over ice.

'Tell me about prison. It wasn't all completely terrible, was it dear?' Mavis had asked, her favourite crystal tumbler poised at her lips. She was elegant in her rose-pink satin dressing gown, her feet shrouded in fluffy mules, but that night Verity had seen in her face the first real signs of ageing.

'Well, it wasn't five-star,' Verity had said with a deprecating laugh. 'And solitary can be a bit lonely.'

'They didn't hurt you, did they.' It was not a question, more a statement, in need of confirmation.

'No Mum, they didn't.' Verity had no desire to add to her mother's distress.

'Thank goodness. I've heard they can be quite harsh.'

'There was one kind police officer,' Verity said, casting about for anecdotes that would release her mother's mind to sleep. 'He arranged for my three-legged bed to be replaced and talked to me sometimes.'

'Oh Verity, what's his name? I'd like to send him a thank you note, you know, for being kind to you.'

'I don't think that would be appropriate Mum. He said his name was Jan Niemand.'

Mavis had looked at her blankly.

'It means John Nobody Mum. He shouldn't have been there. He was breaking the rules. He was just being kind-hearted.'

Verity saw that Mavis did not understand, not any of it and so she tried to think of something else to share.

'One night I heard a man in the cell next to me. I don't know why they had put him in the women's section. Anyway, he wasn't there for long, probably in transit to somewhere else while they waited for a police van or something, but he began to sing. I think he was trying to keep his spirits up.'

'What did he sing?' Mavis asked.

'*The Greatest Love of All.*'

'Oh, I love that song!' Mavis said, putting her whisky glass on the side table and sitting forward. 'Was it the George Benson or Whitney Houston version?'

'Mum!' Verity said, laughing.

'Sorry, how silly of me,' Mavis replied and for the first time in a long time they laughed together, a real belly laugh, at the absurdity of it.

'He gave real vim to the bit that goes, *no matter what they take from me...*'

'*They can't take away my dignity,*' Mavis finished off. 'Oh, Verity! You've given me goosebumps.'

'I know. A prisoner singing to give himself courage and he unwittingly passed some on to me.' She yawned and stretched. 'Now I think I must go and get some sleep, Mum.'

'Yes, you must be exhausted. Good night, dear.'

'Sleep well, Mum,' Verity said, kissing Mavis's forehead.

'You know, I think I just might tonight sweetheart.'

A few days later Verity crept out of the house before light. She put a small suitcase in the back of her car, drove to the airport and waited. A blue Toyota pulled up next to her and a man she did not know climbed out and handed her a plane ticket and false passport. Without looking back, she walked towards the terminal building, focused only on putting one foot in front of the other as she joined the stream of businessmen heading for the red-eye flight to Johannesburg.

At international departures an official took her passport and gave the photo page a cursory glance.

'Going on holiday?'

'Yes,' she said, needing to clear her throat but not daring to, in case it made her sound guilty. He flipped to an empty page and brought down the exit stamp heavily on a smudged page and waved her on.

It was not until the plane had taken off that Verity let down her guard. She scrambled to the toilet, her legs wilting beneath her, and over a metal sink streaked with someone else's spit, she confronted her own haunted face reflected back at her. What she had lost and was losing hit her with force, as did the acknowledgement of what she had done. Her furtive departure, without saying goodbye, would really hurt her mother and sister, and yet she had done just that, simply walked out and left them behind. You've got this, she told herself, but her fists were clenched as tight as her heart.

*   *   *

'Fancy some iced water?' Verity asked Louise, as she turned to the small table next to the braai and lifted off a white cotton crocheted jug cover. 'I recognise this.'

'Ja, it's one Gladys made to keep the flies off. Mave brought it with her when she came to stay with us at the end. She saw it as keeping up standards, like using napkin rings. She used to sit over there at the patio table, watching the birds, weak as a bird herself and always complaining about the heat.'

'You were a saint, Lou. I certainly couldn't have done it.'

'I get that, but what I never understood is why you didn't come back for her funeral.'

Verity picked at a raised fibre along the hem of her dress, trying to marshal a response. "I don't know. I suppose I thought it was too late by then, and I never really got over the feeling that Mum deserted me right at the time when I needed her the most. I was in such pain, and all she could say was, I told you so. How could any mother just abandon their daughter like that Lou?'

'She always asked after you, you know, wanting to know what you were up to. She was proud of you, in her own way.'

'Perhaps. You know when I phoned her after the first

democratic elections, she told me that she and Gladys had voted together and that it had all been very jolly. *I've never agreed with you Verity*, she said, *but I respect you for sticking to your principles, dear*. I tell you, Lou, it was the first time in years I felt her support and I walked out of the international call centre, sat on the steps in Trafalgar Square and cried.'

'She could surprise you like that,' said Lou, turning the lamb chops. 'I heard her one day saying to a friend, *my daughter's flatmate says we should stop complaining about the ANC and help build the new South Africa, and she's Afrikaans!* She utterly adored Hanni even if she couldn't help her prejudices. You know, to her dying day she still referred to her as my housemate.'

'Wow, sweetie, that's a lot of meat you've cooked there,' said Hanneli who had appeared with the salad. 'I hope you've got an appetite, Verity. If not, the dogs are going to be very happy.'

'So, what's it like living here then,' said Verity as they sat down to lunch. 'It seems a nice estate.'

'The main thing is that it's safe, but the facilities are also amazing, gym, tennis courts, huge pool, and grounds to walk the dogs. It's sociable too, with film nights on a Friday and gatherings on Saturdays when we get together with the neighbours.'

'Do you know Hlanganani means let's get together?' Hanneli asked.

'I do. One of the struggle songs was *Hlanganani Basabenzi*, workers unite.'

'Here we go, back to the politics,' said Lou. 'Is that what prompted the visit? Not just here to see your family, back wanting to get involved again?'

Verity looked up from her plate in time to catch Hanni frowning at Louise. Now was not the time to take Lou's bait.

She spooned out some more salad onto her plate and, taking another mouthful, declared it to be truly the best tasting salad she had ever eaten.

'Catching up with any of your old friends whilst you're here then?' persisted Louise. 'Some of them must be in high places now, and I guess, some will have their snouts in the trough.'

'Not all politicians are corrupt,' Hanneli said crossly.

'No and not all old comrades went into politics,' said Verity. 'Coming back has been a tough decision, Lou, and I can't tell you why now. For years I found myself thinking about the people who incarcerated me, just getting on with their lives, people like Kobus Swart swilling beer and turning steaks on his braai, with other people's blood on his hands. What he did is not something that leaves you. It's always been there, haunting me, like Tariq just disappearing off the face of the earth. I want to know what happened to him.'

'Tariq? Good God! After all these years and a long and happy marriage to Sergio and you're still thinking about that prick?'

'Fuck it, Lou,' Verity looked away, her eyes smarting. 'Perhaps coming back was a mistake. I feel like your absent bougainvillea, alien to you.'

'You've been gone a long time,' Hanneli said shooting Louise a warning look and turning to Verity. 'It's so great to have you back and to be able to finally meet you in person. If you need to get yourself some answers, then that's what you have to do, it's your life, after all.'

'It was always about you and your struggle though, wasn't it Verity. You never took our struggle seriously,' Louise said, clearly not done yet.

'What struggle?'

'Exactly. You and Tariq were always banging on about racial

discrimination and class exploitation while our friends were dying of AIDS. It wasn't easy back then. For us the rainbow nation meant being accepted as lesbians, but you never stopped to think about that, did you?'

'Obviously not enough,' Verity said, realising that her sister's resentment went far deeper than being left to care for their needy mother.

'Is that why you didn't want to stay here with us? You don't feel comfortable with our choices? I told you on the phone you'd be welcome.'

'Perhaps because Verity was worried you'd behave like this,' Hanneli said before Verity could protest. 'You've got to move on sweetie. You're the only family each other has got. Come on, now we have the time to give to each other.'

15

Donny van Rooyen was sitting speaking into his mobile phone when Verity entered the Lord Dunkeld Snug at the Piazza. In his knee-length khaki shorts and short-sleeved shirt he looked out of place in the large tartan upholstered armchair, surrounded by Scottish hunting prints.

'Howzit, Verity,' he said, shutting down the call and getting up. 'I recognise you from the photo on your work website. We could sit outside, there's a table by the pool. Soon the evenings will be too cold for it. What will you have?'

'A rock shandy, please.'

'I see,' he nodded. 'So, you're not a drinker?'

'Not at the moment,' Verity answered.

'Very well,' he said, then called over the waiter, ordered their drinks and asked for them to be brought outside. Verity followed him out to the terrace where he held her chair back for her as she sat down. The waiter returned with their drinks and little bowls of peanuts and crisps.

'Well, cheers anyway,' von Rooyen said, raising his glass. He was a large man with the hint of a beer belly who looked even larger with his legs spread and elbows out wide across the table, his hands weathered with liver spots.

'So, Verity, I've been very busy on your behalf but I'm afraid I've not turned up anything on Tariq Randeree. At your suggestion, I got in touch with his cousin, Yasmin Karim. She hasn't seen or heard from him since he left for Swaziland in the eighties, and nor has the rest of the family, which you probably know already. She sends her best by the way and is looking forward to seeing you again.'

'It was a long shot. I would have thought that if she had heard anything she would have contacted me. We were pretty close back in the day, but you know how things go. We just simply lost touch.'

'It happens to us all Verity, life always has a habit of getting in the way.'

'What about Tariq's mother? Did you try speaking to her?'

'No point. Mrs Randeree has dementia, gaga apparently. She's in a care home in Durban. As for the rest of the family, they're all adamant Tariq's dead. They think he was a victim of one of those mystery killings by rogue elements in the security forces back in the day. So, my apologies, on Tariq Randeree it looks like it's a dead end, but I have found Kobus Swart.'

'How? Is he still in Durban?'

'No, but give me a chance,' he said as he took a sip of his Windhoek Lager. 'Ah that's better, nice and cold how I like it. It wasn't too hard finding him, actually. Plenty of old colleagues in the force were more than happy to fill me in. He left the police under a cloud apparently, and after that no one would employ him, not even the more questionable private security outfits.

His wife took him to the cleaners when they got divorced, a domestic abuse case, which doesn't surprise me from what I heard about him. After that he moved to Pretoria, and lived with his sister and brother-in-law for a while before he met a widow at their church, and now he's shacked up with her and living off her widow's pension.'

'Why did he have to leave the police?'

'He faced some sort of disciplinary action, I don't know what it was for, unusual in the security police. He was forced to retire early, just before the generous pay outs whites received to make way for more black police officers when apartheid ended. That must have burnt his arse, though he's managed to land it in the butter again.'

'I want to meet him. I need to eyeball him.'

'It's beyond me why, but you're the boss. I found out which church he goes to in Pretoria. I could take you, it's only fifty kilometres or so from here.' He opened his phone and brought up a map. 'See, the Dutch Reformed Church right there, but can I ask you, why do you want to see a Neanderthal like him?'

'No, you can't but I appreciate the offer to take me there.'

'Okey dokes, I'll pick you up on Sunday morning. It'll be early, I'll text you the time. Now if you don't mind me saying, your skin's getting a bit pink.' His eyes rested on the line where her pale breasts met her newly crimson décolletage. 'I hope you brought sunscreen with you, it's helluva expensive here. We say it's a stealth tax on whites,' he laughed.

'I'll remember to put it on tomorrow,' said Verity, smiling, but adjusting her neckline. 'Did you come up with anything on Viljoen?'

'Now that's a man I can understand you wanting to meet. He was right at the top of National Intelligence, and I have good news. You'll be pleased to know I've come up trumps.'

'Good going, where is he?'

'Well,' said van Rooyen beaming as if she had just awarded him a gold star, 'I figured he would have received a handsome retirement package and there are only so many things rich Afrikaners do with their wealth. One of them is to buy a farm.'

'So, you looked up a register of farm owners and found Viljoen's name?'

'Sort of,' van Rooyen said, looking deflated. 'It was a bit more complicated than that. Viljoen was never one to get his own hands dirty. Sure enough, it turns out his brother-in-law runs the place, and the deeds are in his name, Piet van der Westhuizen. It's probably also a tax dodge of some kind. So, ja, it was more than just flipping through a property register.'

'Well done,' she said, sipping on her Rock Shandy. 'So, what else do wealthy Afrikaners do with their money?'

'They spend a shedload on golf, although to be fair that's not just wealthy Afrikaners, English too, and half the blacks who are now in government.'

'Golf?'

'Ja, and predictably Viljoen also invested in a townhouse on a golf estate in Parys, a very exclusive one, he'll be at one or other place.'

'Parys? It's in the Free State, right?'

'Ja, last time I looked,' van Rooyen said cheerfully. 'It's about a hundred kilometres from Jo'burg so you could do it in a day but better to stay overnight. Parys is fantastic, perfect climate and tons to do, like skydiving from the edge of the crater it sits in, or ziplining across the Vaal River. Okay, your face is telling me that's not your bag. You could just sit with a nice cold glass of wine and admire the famous blue hills and breath in the pure highveld air.

Ag man, I forgot you don't drink wine. You're a hard woman to please. Do you like golf? I could come too, and we could fit in a few holes. I could take you to a draai-en-braai. You should stay at the Riverside Bed and Breakfast. It's beautiful on the banks of the Vaal. The owner's a friend, she'll give you a discount. I'll give her a ring.'

'Slow down,' Verity said, a touch severely. 'I'm going to Parys to speak to Viljoen, not to barn dance.'

A breeze rippled over the surface of the pool, and Verity shrugged her cardigan over her shoulders as she wondered what it would feel like to encounter Viljoen again, the man whose chilly indifference had once sent shivers down her spine.

'Ja, okay, you can go on your own, but you need to be careful,' van Rooyen said. 'Jy krap met 'n kort stokkie aan 'n groot leeu se bal!'

'I'm afraid my Afrikaans is a bit rusty.'

'Literally? You're scratching a big lion's balls with a very short stick. Viljoen doesn't suffer fools.'

'I'll bear that in mind,' Verity said, smiling.

'We'll if you're not up to anything until Sunday, perhaps I could take you out for a bite to eat tomorrow? There's a great steakhouse just down the road.'

'Thanks, but I've got plans,' said Verity, 'I'm meeting up with an old acquaintance.'

'Anyone I would know?'

'Perhaps.'

'We'll you've got my number if you change your mind,' said van Rooyen, as he finished his drink and stood up. 'I'll leave you in peace and see you on Sunday then. Cheers Verity.'

As Donny van Rooyen lumbered from the terrace back through the hotel, Verity leant back in her chair and her thoughts turned to the man she was meeting and their struggle years, when she was caught up in the early days of her romance with Tariq. She had fallen hard after attending the funeral of Agatha Khumalo, when he had stood next to Simeon Sikhakhane, the master of ceremonies, commanding the crowd with his words. When she had met Imran in London he had given her Simeon's details and said that of all the old comrades, he might be the only one who would know anything about Tariq.

*   *   *

At the reception for the World Education Forum Verity had sought out the woman from the British Council who was responsible for the South African delegation.

'Thanks so much for ensuring I got an invitation to this.'

'It was not difficult. Your name was already on the list of people the new Minister wanted to meet,' the woman had said. 'Grab yourself a drink and I'll bring him over.'

Verity lifted a glass of champagne from one of the passing waiters and took a deep swallow as she looked around at the opulent surroundings. She wondered what Imran Malik would make of Lancaster House with its gilded gallery and silken drapes, designed to convey Britain's standing in the world. It would not pass his notice, she thought, that the wealth funding this luxury had been siphoned from the shores of the very countries the British were aiming to impress tonight.

An ill-groomed man in a dishevelled suit appeared before her, and Verity felt the room dwindling to a small circle of which she was inescapably a part.

'Dr Vargas, meet Minister Malik.' The British Council woman pushed Imran forward as if presenting a prize.

'Hello Verity.'

'Oh, you two already know one another?'

'We were once very well acquainted, not so Verity?' Imran had grinned at her through teeth that had suffered from years of imprisonment and neglect.

'It was a long time ago,' Verity said stiffly, draining the remainder of her champagne.

Other guests began to join the group, pushing forward, all keen to talk to the new South African Minister for Education, and Verity backed away, unnerved by how Imran never lost eye contact with her while he shook hands and exchanged greetings with his audience. Feeling the noise level rise, Verity set her empty glass on a passing tray and hurried out, stumbling down the grand staircase to the foyer.

'That lady from the British Council is like a limpet, but I managed to shake her off,' said Imran who had followed her down.

Verity stared at him, the champagne numbing her ability to say all the things she had rehearsed.

'I was surprised you never came back, not once in all those years.'

'Really? If I had returned you'd have been the last person I'd have wanted to see,' she said coldly, wanting to yell foul-mouthed invectives at him. 'I risked everything to get you and Tariq out of the country and then I never heard a peep from either of you, not a single word of thanks. You used me.'

'We used whatever support we could get in those days, Verity.'

'Well, let's say used is still the operative word,' she spat back at him.

'Let me thank you now then, comrade?'

'Don't you dare call me comrade.' An enormous anger had welled up inside her and she had to resist the urge to strike him.

He looked dejected then, the certainty he used to exude now

as depleted as his fragile frame.

'I want to know what happened to Tariq,' she said, regaining her composure.

The guests from the reception had begun to leave and were congregating in the foyer, some edging closer in the hope of another interaction with the minister.

'My hotel is just around the corner,' said Imran, 'It's not the best place for us to talk in here. Will you walk back with me?'

Verity nodded her agreement and went to collect her coat. When she emerged onto the forecourt, she found Imran was stamping his feet against the cold. His eyes were yellowish, and he looked oddly pallid. Taking her arm, as if for support, they weaved their way through the gathering out into Pall Mall. Side by side, they kept pace with each other as taxis and buses rumbled past them.

'Come on then, tell me what happened to Tariq,' said Verity as they walked. 'The last time I saw him was getting into the car with you that night at the Holiday Inn at Ermelo. You were there, you must remember?'

'You have a good memory Verity, perhaps better than mine,' said Imran as he leant up against a lamppost, seeming out of breath. 'The one thing I do know is that Tariq never got into the car with me that night. When the alarm woke me up, he wasn't in our room. I assumed he'd gone to say goodbye to you, so I waited, but when our detail arrived and there was still no sign of him, I couldn't wait any longer. I crossed the border without him, and I never saw him again. It's very possible the security branch killed him or arrested him. When he failed to get in touch a lot of us wondered if he'd been turned. He was quite close to a couple of guys in the security police, picking up bits and pieces of intelligence from them.'

'After what they did to him during interrogation? How can you even think he'd have gone over to their side?'

'Who knows, but if you mix with pigs you sometimes get covered in shit. You can ask Simeon Sikhakhane. We discussed it, often, and he thinks my theory's plausible.'

'Surely you must have considered other possibilities?' Verity wondered how it was possible that two comrades who had been so close could have completely lost contact and for one to consider the other a traitor.

'Of course. He had the kit. He could have left the country.'

'The kit?'

'Disguises, very professional ones. He went in and out of the country often without being detected. Tariq had been earmarked for training in East Germany. That's where he was supposed to be going after getting across the border from Ermelo and a short spell being debriefed in Swaziland.'

'Military training? So, he was a bloody terrorist after all?'

'Oh Verity, one man's terrorist is another man's freedom fighter,' Imran chuckled. 'Problem is, Tariq never pitched up in the GDR either. We knew because their Communist Party was close to our SACP. They were strong backers of Phezulu. I presume you've heard of it?'

A few fat drops of rain began to hit the pavement. Verity took her umbrella out of her bag, unfolded it and was suddenly overcome with a strong desire to draw a line under the conversation. 'What are you really here for Imran? Why did you even want talk to me?' she asked wearily.

'I wanted you to understand that it was not me who let you down,' he said, as he wrenched a beanie from his pocket and pulled it down over his ears. 'It was Tariq who did that. He let me down too, all of us. I knew that one day you would want to know more, and I thought I owed it to you, to maybe try and make up for the things we did that made you feel used, as you put it.'

Imran took out a cigarette from a crushed packet and lit it under the shelter of Verity's umbrella.

'I don't have much time left,' he said, exhaling a plume of smoke and then swivelling back to face her.

'What do you mean?'

'I have pancreatic cancer Verity. I'm not long for this world.' He watched her, waiting for some reaction, and when it didn't come, he continued. 'I wanted to tell you that you were brave and yeah, as you reminded me earlier, to say thank you. All those months in solitary are hard, whatever your skin colour. Also, to say thanks for the other thing. I was on a bit of a crass mission to make up for my lost years in prison,' he said as he reached out and slowly drew his finger along the length of her bare arm.

Verity flinched, his papery touch reminding her of having to do her comradely duty all those years ago. She took a step back, marvelling at the undaunted confidence of deluded men, and the fact that this one could sleep with his own comrade's lover and then blithely refer to it without thought as to what it might do to her.

'Well, I guess this is it then, Imran,' Verity said, 'you've had your say. I hope it helps salve your conscience, but just so you know, you disgusted me back then and you are no better now, taking no responsibility and blaming Tariq for everything. Now I need to leave. As you said yourself, when you mix with pigs you get covered in shit, and you stink of it still.'

Imran coughed out a laugh. 'You always had a way with words Verity. But listen, if anyone one is going to know anything that might help shed some light on Tariq it would be Simeon Sikhakhane. Here, take his card, one of my team got hold of it for me,' he said as he pulled out a business card from the breast pocket of his jacket. 'If you go back to South Africa look him up, and when you do, be sure to give him my regards.'

16

Rosebank Mall had been no more than a small suburban shopping centre when Verity left South Africa, but now it was a vast, brightly lit paean to commerce with a thumping soundscape. She was meeting Simeon Sikhakhane for breakfast at the food-hall which was made up of high-end restaurants and cafes that were separated from the hoi polloi burger bars and fried chicken shacks by a trellis wall of indoor plants and burbling water features.

'Hayiwena, you found it,' Simeon said as he stood to greet her.

Verity was astonished at how this giant of a man had barely changed over all these years, with the same sense of strength and assurance he used to convey, but now with a newfound calm and poise.

'Let's order then we can talk, it's been too long, Verity.'

'I know, and thank you, Simeon.'

'What for? I haven't done anything yet, although breakfast is on me,' he chortled.

'Oh no, I'm picking up the tab, but thanks for agreeing to

meet me. Most of the old comrades have either gone off the radar, ignored my emails, or flatly refused to see me. You could have done the same.'

'Eish, don't take it personally, Verity. I was super pleased at the thought of seeing you again, but not all olds comrades like looking back.'

'Perhaps they thought I was a liability, not to be trusted, and haven't changed their minds.'

'Hayibo, do you really think that?'

'They wouldn't have made me leave if they didn't.'

'That was to protect you from stuff going down at the time, but there were always those who distrusted whites, just because. Many mistakes were made and none of us got everything right.'

'Did you think that of me?'

'I never did, but it wouldn't have mattered what I thought back then. Once the decision was made by the leadership there was no changing minds, and in the case of our cell, the leaders were represented by Imran and his sidekicks in exile. I just remembered the good times we had before your arrest, you were always so strong. I knew you'd handle prison, and you did. And afterwards...I knew you'd be fine again...hoped you would just make the best of your new life.'

The waiter arrived at their table to take their order, and as Simeon scanned the menu Verity thought how in spite of everything they had shared, Simeon hardly knew her. He had no idea what Kobus Swart had done to her or that she had lost her child with Tariq. Even if he did trust her, he would have assumed, like Imran and with some justification, that it was all a lot easier because she was white. She wondered if he was telling her the truth about why she had been forced to leave, and if he'd had a role to play in it.

'I'll have the poached egg on toast and a freshly squeezed orange juice please bru. Verity, what about you?'

'Just a black coffee, it's too early for me to eat.'

The waiter scribbled down their order, took the menus and left.

'Talking of Imran, did you hear he just died? Look, it's in the news this morning.' Simeon slid a copy of *Business Day* towards her.

Verity picked up the paper and studied the article under the headline, *Imran Malik Veteran of the Struggle Dies*. 'He told me he didn't have long when I met him in London,' she said, folding back the paper and passing it over to Simeon. 'He didn't look well, the years weren't kind to him, but he did tell me to look you up if I returned to South Africa anytime and asked me to pass on his regards.'

'That's good of him. We hadn't seen much of each other recently, me being a lowly government official and him being a big deal minister, but he was quite the fighter in the old days, so let's hope they give him a good funeral. It's not like it used to be with hordes of people cramming into a stadium. The number of people who come to see off our heroes is shrinking every year. The youngsters will just say, *Imran who? Move over umkhulu, it's our turn now*. No respect.'

'I suppose it's the same after any war,' Verity said, 'and it's understandable. I see a lot of people are doing very well for themselves.' She gestured to the tables that were filing up around them.

'There's a lot of new wealth. Look there to your right...don't be too obvious...see the man in the Trotsky glasses, sitting at the table with three white businessmen.'

Verity shifted in her seat and casually turned her head in the direction Simeon had indicated.

'His name is Moses Mahlangu. You wouldn't have come across him, but he used to be one of us, worked on our covert assignments supplying false papers, helping people set up new identities. Always under surveillance, but he was good, never got caught, and he was on the side of the poor and the workers. Look at him now sitting there in his Armani suit with a Rolex on his wrist.'

'The movement took care of him then?'

'Eish, you've been away too long Verity. He has nothing to do with it now. If his new friends and associates thought for one minute that he used to be a communist, they would laugh in his face. No, no, no...he is well and truly part of the new elite. He made a ton of money through the Black Economic Empowerment policy when all businesses were legally required to have black executives and shareholders. It was a good idea in theory, but in reality it just made a few very rich. Some like him really milked it. God knows how many companies he is involved with now.'

'You were never tempted by the private sector?'

'No, someone's got to remember the country's poor and provide them with decent services.'

The waiter arrived with their order, and Simeon tucked into his poached eggs with relish. Verity slowly stirred her coffee, waiting for it to cool, and turned again to look over at Moses Mahlangu's table.

'These are good, you don't know what you're missing,' said Simeon, wiping some spilt yoke from the corner of his mouth. 'You're going to have to do the talking while I tuck in. Tell me what brings you back, and what I can do for you?'

'I want to find out what happened to Tariq.' Verity paused and let the statement hang in the air as Simeon looked up from his plate with one eyebrow cocked. 'I grilled Imran, of course, and he said that Tariq was supposed to be on his way to the GDR, but when he never turned up there, or anywhere else, it was thought he may have been captured and turned. He certainly thought that and implied it was a widely held assumption, which he'd discussed on a number of occasions with you.'

'Hawu, that's a lot to take in.' Simeon said as he finished his final mouthful of food. Thoughtfully he wiped his mouth with the serviette and placed hi knife and fork together on his empty plate. 'Imran was a good man, and he made a significant contribution, but he was not the sharpest tool in the box, not like Tariq. You don't want to take everything Imran said at face value.'

'Did you agree with him? Did you think Tariq became an apartheid spy?'

'Listen, I was mad as hell at Tariq when he disappeared. That man was like a brother to me, we were close like this.' Simeon held up his large fingers and crossed them. 'Then he was gone, and nothing. Like you. Anything could have happened. Turned...I always hoped not, but how could any of us be certain.'

'How come you were so close to Tariq? You and I only ever met a few times and he never really talked about you much?'

'None of us talked openly, Verity, you must remember. I didn't know what you were up to, and you didn't know everything Tariq was doing, that was just the way of things. He and I worked together on the movement's communications - '

'Operation Phezulu?'

'You've heard of it...I suppose it is all out there now...well most of it anyway. Yebo, Tariq was key in developing the new system and the whole communications network, he was brilliant at it. I learned a ton from him. He never liked the fact that Imran began using it for MK purposes. When they started drawing on our networks and resources to move arms, including whole shipments from the GDR, he was mad as hell. He would have been pleased to see that the ANC rejected the armed struggle, you know, as part of the negotiations, but furious that they wrapped it all up under the banner of Operation Phezulu. I was pleased he didn't have to see his precious baby thrown out with the military bath water. That communication system did a lot of good. Did you know it was Phezulu that fielded messages between Mandela and the exiled leadership. I feel sad my bru was never properly recognised for what he did.'

'Really? But you talk about him in the past tense. What do you think happened to him? Turned? Dead?'

'I honestly don't know, Verity.'

'So why did Imran think you were a person who would be able to help?'

'Look, I really don't know what happened to him, but I do still have my contacts, not all of them people I necessarily shout about. Imran would have known that.' Simeon drummed his fingers on the table, while he paused to think. 'There's this guy, Kabo Molefi. He was in the security branch in the old days and faced a lot of flak from his community for being impimpi, so he left. I think he was scared he'd end up necklaced with a blazing tyre around his neck. At the time he was well connected, and even more so now he's a successful businessman. After apartheid ended he got a job in local government and saw that money could be made in property development. He shifted to the private sector, so his connections extend all over. I thought he'd have moved to the northern suburbs like Moses Mahlangu over there, but I hear he's still kicking around in Meadowlands, not surprising, he's a real Soweto man. Leave it with me, Verity, and I will see what I can set up.'

With that, Simeon Sikhakhane pushed back his chair in a gesture that declared the conversation was at an end, but his eyes confirmed the old comradeship between them was still there. He enveloped Verity in his strong arms and bound her to him for a moment. They stood together, two battle-scarred veterans of a struggle that had been a victory, although for some it was only a pyrrhic one.

Sitting outside on the terrace reading the *Sunday Tribune,* Verity sensed a presence and looked up to see an exhausted Donny van Rooyen looking down at her.

'Goeie môre.'

'Hello, are you okay?'

'Forgive me but I'm feeling a bit buggered, I was at the vet all night with Koekie, our family dog. At one point I thought we were going to have to put the old girl down, but she's going to be okay.'

'So sorry to hear that, Donny. Are you sure you want to drive to Pretoria? I'm fine going on my own, and I need to drop in to see Yasmin on my way back.'

'My wife's got it all in hand now and I'm good to go. I can drop you at Yasmin's on our return, and anyway, it's time I had a word with my maker,' he said with a snort of laughter. 'Let's go.'

Verity followed him out and when they reached his Ford Ranger he helped her up into the passenger seat.

'Are you sure you want to do this?' he asked. 'The man's a fokking doos. Sorry for the language, but it's true. You don't know what he's capable of, that oke wouldn't need to be hungry to turn your pet dog into boerewors. I don't like the idea of you squaring up to a character like him, and not on your own.'

'Well, luckily it's not up to you,' Verity said with a grin, 'and I won't be on my own. You'll be there, although I want to speak to him by myself.'

The relatively short drive seemed to take forever. Van Rooyen talked non-stop about his dog, how much he loved her, how dogs really were man's best friend, and all the while Verity could only think about what lay ahead. She asked herself if she was really up for this and began to question the wisdom of her decision. Just when she was about to tell Donny to turn back, he pulled into a large car park.

'Here we are, Verity. You ready for this?'

Churchgoers mingled outside the Dutch Reformed church on what was a clear and sunny morning. Verity watched as families arrived in clusters then split up around the forecourt. Men with mullets took last drags of their cigarettes, boys pushed each other about the shoulders while giggling teenage girls in their Sunday best watched them shyly. Young mothers converged on one another, toddlers with bed-head hair hanging on their skirts, and the older women, who were uniformly dressed in hats and pastels, their handbags over marbled forearms, handed out the order of service from the shade of the portico.

Then there he was, Kobus Swart with a woman on his arm.

They split up and he joined the smokers. Bubbles of bile rose in Verity's throat as she took him in from where they sat in the car. He looked much the same except for the swollen pelmet of fat hanging over his trousers, and the fact he was now bald apart from a grubby grey crescent below the crown. Thick tufts thrust their way out of the neck of his shirt as if that was where the rest of his hair had migrated.

The church bells began to ring and those gathered outside started making their way inside.

'Let's just give them a minute,' said van Rooyen, 'then we'll find ourselves a pew near the back.'

Verity watched as Swart stubbed out his cigarette and located his wife waiting in the portico. Donny, opened the car door on Verity's side, helped her down, then took her arm and walked her to the entrance. Every step felt like torture, and she thought the thumping of her heart would drown out the sound of the bells. She closed her eyes and hoped she would get through the service without throwing up.

'That's him,' said van Rooyen, scanning the backs of the heads in front of them, some bowed, some still locked in last minute conversations. Swart was talking to a woman with a beehive, which moved in unison with the incline of her neck as she listened. 'That must be his wife.'

The dominee raised a hand and the murmured conversations subsided. With the first hymn, van Rooyen began to translate in Verity's ear.

God sorg vir die mossies *God cares for the sparrows*
God sorg vir die diere *cares for the animals*
God sorg vir die plante *cares for the plants*
God sal sorg vir jou *God shall care for you*
Is jy dalk bekommerd *Why are you worried*
God sal sorg vir jou *God shall surely care for you*

A woman in the pew in front turned and scowled at him. Verity told him it was fine, she was getting the gist. She was quite content to see out the service in partial incomprehension.

When the final blessing was given, 'may the Lord keep you and give you peace,' van Rooyen chuckled and whispered, 'there'll be no peace for the wicked today.'

'Amen,' Verity agreed, but her nervous heart was chaffing.

She caught up with Swart as he was heading for the smokers. Through pressed lips and rising panic, she said, 'can I have a word?' For a strangely static second it seemed Swart did not know her. 'Verity Saunders,' she said.

'Juffrou Saunders! What the hell are you doing here?' he asked, something hardening in his eyes.

'I came to talk to you,' she said, with a shiver of reluctance but not dropping her gaze.

He looked abruptly towards the woman with the beehive who was deep in conversation across the lawn then pulled Verity towards the church. She nodded to van Rooyen, indicating that she was okay, and followed Swart back inside. The central lights had been switched off and the interior was now dim and shadowy. Verity fought the instinct to flee.

'What do you want?' Swart growled.

'I want you to listen to what I have to say and then answer my questions. Did you enjoy your job?'

'It was a job,' he shrugged.

'Did you ever seek forgiveness for what you did in the course of your work?'

He looked at her bemused, fumbling with his cigarette lighter. The sight of his nicotine-stained fingers was painfully memorable, but somehow it gave her resolve.

'Well? We're here in the presence of the guy upstairs who looks after the little sparrows and animals. What did your god think of your antics?'

'Listen man, just leave me alone, I've had a kak time. My wife buggered off with another bloke, and my kids ignore me. I'm just getting back on my feet.'

'Are you expecting me to feel sorry for you?' Verity asked, feeling her resolve harden. 'Did you get satisfaction from what you did, and you know what I'm talking about?'

'I did what I was told,' he said sulkily, glancing at the floor.

'You all say that. Just following orders. But you added your own special spice to it, didn't you? You went beyond the call of duty.'

Kobus Swart looked at her blankly. Verity felt the church walls closing in on her. Determined not to allow his incomprehension to derail her, she conjured up the horrific images she had carried with her for her entire adult life, of him thrusting into her, the stench of his breath, and then the lifeless body of her child cradled in her arms.

'You are deeply depraved,' she said, her voice rising.

'Sssh man.' He leaned towards her, and she caught the familiar whiff of Klipdrift brandy on his breath.

She knew that stench from when he barked inane questions at her as she stood swaying on a brick. She knew it from those confined journeys in the elevator to the seventh floor, and she knew it from when it burnt her face when he pinned her down in her cell.

'And what about what you did to Tariq? Do you still have that cattle prod?'

'Tariq Randeree was a stubborn coolie, so ja, we gave it to him a bit more than others,' he said, appearing to settle comfortably on this explanation.

'It wasn't *we* though, it was *you*!' she hissed, jabbing a finger into his barrel chest.

'Okay! If you say so,' he hissed back. 'What's it to you anyway?

I never hurt you.'

'That's not how I remember it. Tell me you're a cunt.'

'What?'

'Say it. Say I'm a cunt!' she said icily.

'Keep your voice down,' he said, scanning the pews as if in search of an out.

'You thought you'd blind me with that flashlight, but I'd know your brandy breath anywhere, and I recognised your onyx ring when you shook yourself off.'

There was a shuffle on the doormat at the porch. 'Are you hiding from me Kobus?' his beehived wife trilled.

'Wait for me outside,' Swart barked, then turning back to Verity, said, 'look, I admit, it got a bit out of hand.'

'Not it, Kobus, you. You got very out of hand. I want you to say it, say I'm a cunt like you said to me when you raped me.' Verity spoke with a certain recklessness now, not caring if his wife heard.

'We'd been drinking, you'd been fokking uppity during interrogation. We just thought we'd teach you a bit of a lesson.' One hand clutched at his Marlborough Lights, the same hand that had helped push her legs apart.

'Drinking made it okay, did it?'

'Those were different times. Can we just stop this now, man?'

'Not until you tell me you're a cunt.'

'Shit. Okay, I'm a cunt,' he whispered. 'Enough already.'

'No, because I'm afraid there's more. As a result of your brutal rape, I lost the only child I ever carried.'

The church door banged open and Swart's wife glided up to them.

'Do your church friends and your dominee know your husband's a rapist?' Verity fumed, addressing her. Turning to

Swart again she yelled, 'and what would they think if they knew your actions killed my unborn baby?'

'Look, I'm sorry about the miscarriage,' Swart said, then looking at his wife, 'let's get out of here.'

'Good idea,' she replied, stoney faced. 'We need to get back for lunch.' Then taking Swart's hand she pulled him out of the church.

Verity shook with a mixture of rage and satisfaction. I've done it, she thought, but they just walked away as if it meant nothing to them. Leaving the dark interior behind she stood on the threshold of the portico and let her eyes adjust to the glare of the late morning sun. She watched as Kobus Swart took out his cigarettes, lit one for himself and then one for his wife. They exchanged a few words then walked back over to her. Verity watched as they slowly approached her, detecting in Swart's movements a shadow of calculation.

'You should know something,' he said with a sly twist of his mouth, 'we're better off with our own kind. Perhaps I did you a favour. You know your child would have been a half-caste?'

'That half-caste child would have been my child,' Verity shouted at Swart, 'and Tariq was not a coolie, he was an anaesthetist. He took away pain. He didn't inflict it. Tell that to your bloody God in Heaven.'

'Kom Kobus, she has no respect for our Lord,' said Swart's wife, giving Verity a backward glance as mild as a glass of milk.

Verity leant back against the church wall and gave into a feeling of something adjacent to defeat. She stayed there and watched as the carpark emptied of people until the only person left was Donny van Rooyen, leaning patiently against the side of his Ford Ranger.

'Did it go okay?' he asked.

'That man has no conscience. I don't know what I thought

I would achieve but what I said didn't affect him, not one iota.'

'Sorry, man, shit floats,' Donny said, patting Verity's arm. 'Come on, let's get out of here. I'll drop you at Yasmin's.'

On the journey back Verity stared hypnotically at the pale patina of the grassy banks along the dual carriageway. Kobus Swart gave Afrikaners a bad name, she thought, yet for every Swart there was someone like her sister-in-law Hanni, who was the kindest person on this earth. Even among the police, there were kind Afrikaners, she reminded herself, like the young officer who had swapped her three-legged bed for a good one, or Donny van Rooyen sitting beside her right now, whistling *Suikerbossie* tunelessly through his teeth.

Donny van Rooyen drew up outside a large white double storey house in Greenside and switched off the engine. 'I'm happy to wait here for you if you'd like.'

'No, it's fine, I can get a taxi back,' said Verity, as she got out of the car, 'but thanks so much for today.'

'No hassle. If you'd like to try that steakhouse I told you about I could pick you up tomorrow around seven.'

'Why not? Thanks,' said Verity, as she closed the car door.

She turned towards the house and inhaled deeply. She and Yasmin had been so close and shared so much, yet a lot of water had passed under the bridge since then, she thought as she made her way up the brick path and climbed the black stoep steps to ring the doorbell.

'Hiya, kiddo!' said Yasmin as she flung the door open and threw her arms around Verity. 'It's so darned good to see you again. Come on inside and out of heat. I hope you don't mind but I ask folk to take their shoes off.'

Verity slipped off her pumps and followed Yasmin barefoot across the polished parquet floor, a knot of emotion in her throat.

'Your house is amazing,' she got out, wishing she could think of something to say that was closer to the enormity of what she was feeling.

'Yeah I'm lucky, and it's nice to have the room for when the kids come, but most of the time it's just me rattling around here on my own. What can I get you?'

'A glass of water would be great.'

'Sparkling? Make yourself at home and I'll bring it through.'

Yasmin returned, handed Verity a glass of ice and bubbles, and showed Verity into a dining room that appeared to double as a study.

'It's where I prefer to do my work. It's cooler downstairs and closer to the kitchen to make a cup of coffee. There was a study upstairs, and I hoped if we got back together Todd would use it, but since the divorce I turned it into another guest room for when the kids come and visit. Now give me a minute. I've knocked us up some lunch,' said Yasmin as she disappeared into the kitchen. 'I'm a vegetarian these days,' she shouted back through, 'I hope that's okay.'

While she waited Verity scanned the titles on Yasmin's bookshelves. Most were testimony to her career in public health, as a medic and a feminist intellectual. She spotted the spine of Robin Norwood's *Women Who Love Too Much*, and realised she had no way of knowing her old friend as a wife and mother, let alone someone who had lived through a divorce.

'Sit yourself down, we've a lot of catching up to do Verity Saunders,' Yasmin said, returning with a tray laden with bread, cheese and salad and putting it down at one end of the oak dining table with its burn rings and water marks from family meals past.

'Verity Vargas.'

'Vargas, sorry, old habits and all that. I was so sorry to hear about your husband...'

'It's been tough, but it sounds like it has been hard for you as well.'

'It's a woman's life Verity...and how strange and unpredictable it can be. Like this bloody country. Can you believe race is still on the agenda and Indians and Coloureds are still stuck in the middle. Not white enough in the past, not black enough now. Anyway, we're not here to talk politics, despite past form. It's great to see you back. How long has it been? Twenty years? More?'

'Closer to thirty, and it's fantastic to see you too. You haven't changed a bit.'

'Well thank you kindly, a few more grey hairs but hey, don't we all. You are looking great yourself. So, what prompted the great return then, I take it you're not just here for a holiday?' asked Yasmin as she sat down at the table and started to slice the bread.

'I don't know, not really. I wanted a go at finding out the truth. I thought I'd put my time in the struggle behind me, but after Sergio died, for some reason it all came flooding back. Sergio always warned me things as momentous as that could not just be left to lie. But what about you? How's the family? I have such wonderful memories of us sitting round and sharing dinner with your Ma and Aziz.'

'They were the best of times,' said Yasmin, smiling and inclining her head. 'Look at you, if only they could also be here to see you again. They were always so fond of you. Ma didn't manage too well after Zizi died. How long ago was that now? It must be fifteen years.' She slid a plate over to Verity. 'Here, get stuck in. I hope you like the bread. I baked it myself.'

Verity took a slice. It was warm and brown with a dark crust.

'And your Ma, how is she now?'

'You know, surviving. She's in a care home in Durban. It was a tough decision, but after my divorce I just couldn't cope having her here anymore, she'd got so frail and forgetful and was lonely with me out at work all day. At least she's with her sister now. Did I say they're both in the same place? Although Auntie Bibi isn't great company. She has advanced dementia. Poor woman, she never got over Tariq's death.'

Verity paused in the middle of serving herself some salad, the spoons hovering above her plate. 'So, you think he is dead?'

'Come on Verity. Don't tell me you still think my cousin is alive? 'I remember those ever-hopeful phone calls you'd make from London, but none of us heard anything from him after your arrest. Of course, we hoped, for years we clung on to the merest glimmer of it. But nothing, and you can't carry on like that, look what it did to Auntie Bibi. She never accepted it. When I go to the home to see Ma and her, she sometimes thinks I'm him. But there's no way he could still be alive. You have to let it go, my old friend.'

Verity cut into a piece of Camembert and scraped it on a cracker, trying to ignore the mild rebuke and feeling of emptiness that was accumulating in the pit of her stomach.

'Is that the only reason you came back?'

'It's not just about Tariq. Obviously I wanted to see my sister and old friends, like you, as well,' Verity said, pleased to change the subject. 'And I wanted to confront those bastards who harmed me in prison. Sergio always thought I should do it, rather than punching cushions.' Verity gave a hollow laugh. 'Now he's gone...you know...I just thought he might be happy that I am finally listening to him.'

'Gawd kiddo, why pick the scabs off old wounds now? Isn't it a bit like stalking an old boyfriend who dumped you?'

'You mean Tariq?'

'No, South Africa. I was speaking metaphorically. Let sleeping dogs lie, let them wallow in their own vinegar?'

'Vinegar's a preservative.'

'Touché,' Yasmin laughed. 'This conversation feels like old times.'

'Talking about old times, I saw Imran in London before I came back.'

'Oh good, so you saw him before he died. That was so sad, just when they'd finally given him his own ministry. He came to Aziz's funeral, you know. He was always good to the family and behaved almost like a second son to Auntie Bibbi.'

'He always did what he thought was best,' said Verity, choosing her words carefully as she sliced into some more cheese. She decided not to say how he had cast aspersions on Tariq's loyalty to the cause. 'I did some digging around before I left London. I never knew how much Tariq had done, he always kept so much to himself. But I found out that he played a much bigger role in the struggle than I for one thought.'

'Well, he was the gifted one in the family, so it shouldn't surprise us.'

'Did you know he raised funds for the ANC in Europe?'

'I didn't.' Yasmin's eyes narrowed. 'Tell me more.'

'Did you know he was key to building up the communications network for the movement, a kind of proto-digital system?'

'Well, he was always messing round with computers and disks He was a brilliant man, and a good one, Verity.'

'Maybe.'

'What do you mean, maybe? I get that you were hurt by his disappearance but let's not speak ill of the dead.'

'If he's dead.'

Come on Verity, I don't want to have this conversation. I want to keep the good memories and to live out more happy times. We've all lived through too much darkness.'

Verity fell silent and pushed salad leaves around her plate, keeping her eyes focused on the battle-scarred family table.

'Ok then, you've obviously got something on your chest. Spit it out,' said Yasmin as she gently placed her hand on Verity's arm. 'You want to talk, so talk, and then we can sit and have a peaceful cup of tea in the garden.'

'When I was in prison...' Verity, put down her fork and steeled herself. 'When I was in prison they played me recordings they had made from wire taps...'

'That old interrogation technique, go on.'

'You always doubt whether they are real or not, but when you hear the voices there is no doubt they are real, no matter how much you don't want them to be. In one session...well...they played a tape of Tariq and Amira together...you know, properly together.'

'Amira?'

'Yes, Amira. I couldn't bear it Yas, it broke my heart.'

'Amira, the daughter of the Motalas?'

'I think so.'

'But Tariq was only ever interested in you.'

'I can only tell you what I heard.'

'It was a long time ago Verity, and even if he had, there would have been nothing there, nothing in it. She wasn't his type. Super religious, still is. She's always just at home looking after the kids. I can't imagine Tariq being properly interested in her.'

'You still see her?'

'Now and again, she only lives a couple of blocks away.'

'And she's happily married to someone else?'

'I don't know if she's happy, Verity.'

'But she has children?'

'Two teenage boys, I think?'

Verity dug a thumb nail into the flesh of her palm, an old familiar sting of hurt rising in her throat like a living thing. It was not envy or even akin to it, but rather the pain of wondering yet again what little Owen would have been like if he had survived.

Donny was leaning against his Ford Ranger sucking at a disposable vape when Verity came out of the hotel. When he saw her walking towards him, he pocketed it. 'You look nice,' he said, 'and happier.'

'I'm fine,' she said, brushing away his kindness. 'But you were right, Swart's a flipping Neanderthal. But it was lovely to catch up with Yasmin.'

'That all went well then?'

'Just like we'd never been apart. Funny how you can slip right back into it with old friends.'

'I'm pleased for you Verity,' he said, once more helping her up into the passenger seat.

When he turned on the ignition Dolly Parton blared out of the speakers, a song about a child whose puppy had died. He quickly ditched it.

'You don't need to do that, Dolly's great, although maybe that track is one to put a dampener on a fun night out.'

Donny hooted. 'Funny, I had you down as a classical music buff.'

'I have eclectic taste.'

'Electric?'

No, I mean I like all sorts of music, classical, rock, folk, country, especially world music.'

'Ag ja, like Bono Visto Social Club?'

'Buena Vista Social Club,' she corrected, ever the pedant.

Just around the corner he pulled up into an empty space and raised a hand in thanks to the car guard who had been elaborately waving his arms to direct him. He put some coins into the man's cupped hand, promising more on their return, then leapt round the car to open Verity's door.

'This is two minutes from the hotel, we could have walked,' Verity said.

'Ja, nee but this is South Africa. Welcome to Sir Loin's Steak House, it's the whole medieval shtick. I recommend you have the fillet. It's so tender it will melt in your mouth.'

The waiter appeared with large menus attached to planks. Donny waved his away. 'I know what I'm having, my friend, the Friar Tuck T-bone, well done, with fat chips and a Windhoek lager to wash it down. And what about you, Verity?'

'The Sister Sarah fillet, medium, a green salad and a Rock Shandy please,' said Verity to the waiter, then turned back to Donny and said, 'why don't you tell me a bit about yourself?'

'Nothing to tell, really. I'm just a bloke.'

'There must be more to you than that.'

'Not a lot.' He grinned. 'What about you? How old are you if you don't mind me asking?'

'I do as a matter of fact. How old are you?'

'Firmly over the hill but not yet out to graze. Anyway, they say the fifties are the new forties.'

'I look forward to finding out,' Verity said with a grin.

'Can I ask you something that's been puzzling me? Why do you have a British accent if you grew up here.'

'I suppose because I've lived in London for thirty odd years, but also I had immigrant parents, so as a child I sounded like them. My sister who is much younger and was born here sounds more South African. She was also spared the elocution lessons I had to endure. My mother was worried I'd develop South Africa's dreaded flat vowels.'

'Dreaded, hey?'

'If I said I'm going to the bioscope she would say, *it's not the bioscope, it's the cinema.* By the time my sister came along she'd just say, *goodbye dear, have a nice time.* My friends sometimes pronounced my name *Virity*, that's the dreaded flat vowel, and my mother would go mad. She'd say, *it's not Virity, it's Verity, E spells eh, not 'ih.'*

'What did you say to that?'

'I said, *what about England?*'

'Jeez, you must have been a handful.'

The waiter arrived back with their order. Donny cut into his steak and chewed vigorously.

'Beryl, my wife, and I went to England once, when our girls were old enough to be left.' He spoke as he chewed. 'We did a trip round seven European cities in a fortnight.'

'Did you like it?'

'Amsterdam was nice, and we liked the food in Rome, although jeez they drive like maniacs there. But England, not really. Sorry if that offends you. Mind you, we only went to London and Edinburgh.'

'Edinburgh's in Scotland.'

'Wherever, all I know is it rained all the time and was dark by the middle of the afternoon, and it was blerrie cold outside and too hot inside with the heating. I remember I went to open the hotel window, and it had been painted shut. Can you believe it? And they had also painted right over a dead fly on the windowsill. You could see its shape under the gloss.'

Verity wiped away laughter tears with her serviette.

'Do you prefer South Africans or the English?' he asked, lowering his fork, and wiping grease from his chin.

'Hard question,' Verity said, picking at her salad. 'South Africans are a bit rough-edged, but I like that they're straight-talking. You pretty much know where you stand with them. The English can be a bit too smooth, and you don't always catch the ripples underneath.'

'You're going to have to explain,' Donny said, putting down the T-bone he'd begun stripping clean with his teeth.

'Once I remember there was a disagreement over something at work. It was only when I got home and thought about the meeting that I realised it had been a real contretemps, because everyone sounded so polite at the time.'

'A real what?' He held up two fingers about a centimetre apart, as if to say his understanding of what she had said would fit in no more than that space.

'A contretemps, you know, a dispute.'

'Can you try and speak in English so this poor uneducated Afrikaner bloke can understand?'

They carried on in this light-hearted vein until the restaurant began emptying out and Verity joked about South Africa's eight thirty watershed.

'Hell yes, my bedtime,' Donny said, playing along. 'Now are you all set for tomorrow? Are you sure I can't take you there? Any excuse to go to Parys.'

'No thanks Donny, I could do with some peace and quiet on the drive.'

'Suit yourself,' he said, reaching inside his jacket pocket. 'Here are the instructions on how to reach Viljoen's farm, and this is a card for my friend's guest house. I'll ring ahead tomorrow morning for you and book.'

'Much appreciated.'

'And after you get back, who else do you have on your list for me?'

'This is the last one, Donny. I'm going to stop going after the bad guys after Viljoen. Yasmin said I should stop picking at the scab and I think she's right. If I don't I think I'll never heal.'

'Sounds like your old friend knows what she's talking about. Too many things can drag us back to the past, particularly in this crazy country.'

'Thank you, Donny for everything you've done. You've been a real help. I mean that. I don't think I could have faced Swart if it wasn't for you. And thank you for a lovely evening, it's been fun switching off and just talking about normal things for a while.'

'Ja, it was lekker. Now let me get the bill and I'll drive you back to the hotel.'

'I think I'll walk. It will probably be quicker,' laughed Verity.

Donny went up to the bar to pay, patting every pocket before reaching inside his jacket for the one containing his wallet. As he stood waiting, he began chatting to a man sitting on a stool nursing a drink. Verity watched as their middle-aged backs moved, in casual comfort to the rhythm of their conversation.

'A friend of yours?' she asked when he returned to the table.

'An acquaintance. To be honest with you, he's been pretty good at giving me some leads on the guys I've found for you. He works here in Jo'burg for a private security company, but he used to work for the security police back in the day. I asked him along tonight in case you wanted to speak to him.'

'What's his name?'

'Deon, Deon Openshaw. A nice enough chap to be honest with you.'

'Would you introduce him to me before you go?'

'Ha, and here were you saying you were letting it all go after Viljoen.'

'I've not seen Viljoen yet.'

'Come on then,' laughed Donny, 'but don't you go stealing my sources.'

They walked up to the bar together and Donny tapped Deon on the shoulder. 'Hey, man, this young lady would like a chat with you. And you go easy on her, she has me looking out for her,' he said as he slapped the man on the back. 'Don't stay up too late with Deon here, you've a big drive tomorrow.' He wrapped Verity in a hug and she felt his beer belly pressing into her. 'Just give me a call if you need anything else, or if you change your mind and want me to drive you tomorrow.'

'Thanks Donny,' she said as she prised herself out of his embrace.

He winked at her, patted Deon on the shoulder by way of farewell, and made his way out of the restaurant.

Verity sat down on the stool next to Donny's source and stared into a pair of fiercely blue eyes framed by rimless glasses. She examined the thick head of silver hair, and the whorls of hair on his forearms, but it was when her eyes alighted on his enormous watch that recognition dawned. There was no mistaking it, Deon Openshaw was the captain who had interrogated her all those years ago in the prison in Durban.

'So, Verity Saunders, you want to talk to me. Can I get you a drink? No? So, what can I do for you? No, don't tell me. Let me guess. You're writing a history. I get so many academics and writers wanting to interview me these days, from all over the place, America, Sweden, Germany.'

Verity could not believe who she was looking at and struggled to take in his words.

'Cat got your tongue? I remember you being full of cheek.'

'It's you...you interviewed...I mean interrogated me...you...'

'So what history is it you are writing then?'

'I'm not writing a history,' said Verity, recovering her composure. 'I'm just trying to understand the past, a past that you were a part of, a very nasty part.'

'I've been part of many people's nasty pasts.' Openshaw gave a deep laugh. 'If you're here to confront me about that, you wouldn't be the first. One day, two black guys with guns sauntered into my office and asked me what I was going to do about having banged them up. They were after money of course. I told them what I told the TRC when I testified. We were fighting a civil war and were just on different sides, like you and me, Verity.'

'A war in which you bastards held all the power,' she said, trembling with shock and rage. 'Did you ever think what it must have been like for me in solitary confinement, imprisoned without charge, subject to your interrogation at whim? Was it fair play in war to have recorded my mother's phone calls and played them back to me? Can you even imagine what it's been like carrying that fear, that anger, for over thirty years?'

'Did you really think of me as your enemy?' Against Verity's emotion, Openshaw was studiously casual.

'Well you clearly thought of me as yours.'

'In as much as I would have done anything within my power to stop the ANC in its tracks, and that included you, Verity. So yes, you could say you were my enemy. What else do you want me to say? Did you expect anything different? To fall at your feet and apologise? You were all the same to me, you and your friends, Imran Malik and Tariq Randeree. You really got in with the wrong crowd there. You still in contact?'

'Imran's dead and no one's heard from Tariq since back then. But you already know that, right?' Imran told me you tried to recruit Tariq.'

'You should take a leaf out of my book Verity. I stay away from the news nowadays, It's all so depressing. I just let sleeping dogs snore away.'

'Did you recruit him? Did Tariq come over to your side?' Verity could feel her anger swelling.

'We tried to recruit a lot of people Verity, but Tariq was never a man to be swayed to our side. He should have done, it might have turned out better for him and it certainly wasn't for want of trying. He would have been a very valuable asset to our national intelligence, but he consistently refused. I admired him actually and told him so. I said, *Tariq Randeree, you'd be a credit to any government you served but I'm not about to let you bring down mine.* In the end it was him who played us, and whatever the ANC likes to put about, we didn't kill him either.'

'So what happened to him then?'

'Fuck knows.' Openshaw said, squinting at her. 'We knew he was messing about with some kind of technology, it was only later that Operation Phezulu all came out. That's normally what the historians who come to see me are interested in, especially the Germans. He shouldn't have got mixed up with Imran and all of that. Nice piece of kit though, who'd have thought Tariq Randeree would have been the one to set up a hotline to East Berlin, although a fat lot of good those commies did him in the end.'

'When you interrogated me, you said Tariq never reached the

safe house. Did he make it across the border, did you pick up his whereabouts after the raid? You must have had the Swazi guards in your pockets, so they would have told you.'

'They were paid fuck all, so why wouldn't they work for us? But that border was like a sieve, contraband goods, small arms, people trafficking, terrorists, the lot, all coming and going, I wouldn't know about it all. And no, we never picked up on Tariq Randeree again.'

'Then what happened to him?'

'Hmmm...' Openshaw swilled down the last of his whisky. 'I've no idea Verity. I can't help you with that. It might be best to think of him as collateral damage. As I said, it was war.'

Before Verity could press him any further, Openshaw slapped down a note on the bar and casually walked away. At the door of the restaurant, he paused briefly, turned to glance at her, shook his head, then left.

20

From the elevated highway skirting Johannesburg's city centre, Verity picked out familiar landmarks: the old stock exchange building and Eleven Diagonal Street, a wonder in its day with its glass panels designed to resemble a multi-faceted diamond, which to Verity now looked somehow diminished. She took the slipway onto the N1 towards Bloemfontein and wound down the window, happy to be on the open road, drumming her fingers to Yvonne Chaka Chaka's *Burning Up* playing on the car radio. There was something liberating about being alone behind the wheel of a car and thoughts of Swart and Openshaw receded with every mile that ticked away.

When Verity arrived in Parys and found the Riverside Bed and Breakfast, she got out of the car, took her case from the back seat, arched her aching back and took in a large draught of highveld air. A woman who looked like a middle-aged Barbie doll came through a gate in a hedge that shielded the main house from the car park. She was dressed from head to painted toe in Schiaparelli pink, matching the bows on the heads of the flurry of Yorkshire Terriers at her feet, whose tongues were also obligingly pink.

'Renata van der Merwe,' she said, putting out her hand. 'You must be Verity. I hope the drive was smooth?'

'Very easy thank you, it only took me a couple of hours.

'Don't mind my pooches, they don't bite. Off you go now, back inside. You've said hello to Verity.' She spoke to the dogs as if they were her children and they obediently scampered back through the gate. 'Here, let me get someone to take your case and I'll show you your room.'

'It's fine, I've got it.'

'Okay, this way.'

Verity followed her down a crazy-paving path to a row of motel style rooms, which she guessed would have been converted from what once had been the servants' quarters. The accommodation was made up of a sitting room, with a small kitchenette, and a bedroom with an on-suite bathroom. The décor was entirely maroon, the curtains, the throw on the bed, the towels, and the crocheted antimacassar against the back of a chair. Even the potpourri, faded under a light film of dust, had once been burgundy.

'You like it?'

'Everything matches,' Verity said brightly.

'Thanks, hey. I designed it myself. 'Here's the key, enjoy your stay. The info you need is in here.' She handed Verity a plastic binder with emergency numbers, the Wi-Fi password, and leaflets for local restaurants.

Verity put her case in the bedroom and not wanting to spend a minute longer in the oppressive room, she decided to head straight out of town towards Viljoen's farm. As she drove, following the directions Donny had given her, streetlights gave way to electricity pylons, then to grain silos and windmills. When she saw a sign to Uitkyk Plaas she turned onto the dirt farm road and drove along an avenue of blue gums. She passed labourers' barracks with lines of washing outside and old tyres heaped in the long grass. After rounding some high-sided concrete water tanks, she arrived abruptly at the main farmhouse and her courage immediately deserted her. Just as she was thinking about turning around and getting out of there, a man up a ladder fixing a gutter saw her, waved and started to climb down. Okay, she thought, it's now or never, I guess.

Two Rottweilers bound into view as the man reached the bottom of the ladder and made his way to her car. Verity opened the window and immediately the dogs bared their teeth and began to bark. The man called them to heel and they fell silent, still quivering aggressively at his side.

'Kan ek jou help?' he asked.

'Ja, asseblief, maar praat jy Engels?'

'Ja, I speak a little.'

'Thank you. I'm looking for Anton Viljoen.'

'You're in the right place.' He wiped his hands on the back of his trousers and stepped forward. 'Piet van der Westhuizen. I'm Anton's brother-in-law.'

'Verity Vargas,' she said, getting out of the car. 'I knew Anton many years ago, although he will remember me as Verity Saunders. I was just passing ...' Verity did not know where her shamefaced explanation had emerged from, or why Piet van der Westhuizen could not see she was quivering more than his Rottweilers.

'You know Anton had a serious stroke? Ja, he can't live alone anymore, so he's in the big house with us. You won't get a word out of him, but he'll be pleased to see you. Let me call my wife.'

He strode up to the house, stepping over more lolling dogs on the stoep. Hesitantly Verity followed, edging past the Rottweilers, who stood passive but alert at the door.

'Elize!'

A birdlike woman appeared in the hall, securing her hair into a bun coiled at the nape of her neck.

'This is Verity, a friend of Anton's. She didn't know about his stroke.'

'Ag shame, ja it's a terrible thing,' she said, regarding Verity with polite enquiry.

'I'm not really a friend,' Verity hastily explained, any earlier confidence rapidly draining away. 'We knew each other in the course of his work. It was a long time ago. I think I'd better leave.'

'Nonsense, he'd love a visitor and you'd be doing me a favour. I'm making cakes for the church bazaar and I've had no time for Anton today. Just sit with him. It will be a fresh face. Come on, I'll show you through and get you some tea.'

The room was large and smelt of antiseptic. Apart from a hospital bed angled towards the window, and the view of hills outside, the furniture was all antique, including a highly polished oak commode in one corner. A posy of fresh flowers sat on a side table next to a wingback armchair, and Verity's first glimpse of Viljoen was of his mottled feet resting on a needlepoint footstool. Her stomach pitched at the sight.

Rounding the wing-back with its plastic arm protectors, Verity regarded the slumped figure of the man who had once dictated her life course with little more than a slight incline of his head. What in hell's name was she supposed to do with him now? She had waited too long for this confrontation, she thought, as he stared back at her through rheumy eyes, how knowingly she couldn't tell.

Elize had disappeared and Verity just stood there mesmerised by a trail of saliva that ran down one of the deep, raw cracks that bracketed Viljoen's mouth. She pushed down a tinge of sympathy and reminded herself that when he had been all-powerful, there had been no moral distinction between him, the man who gave the orders, and the ones who had carried them out.

'You remember Verity?' said Elize as she re-entered the room carrying a tray of tea. 'It's so nice of her to come and visit, not so Anton?' She spoke in that sing-song voice people reserve for small children, dogs and the infirm. She set down the tray on an occasional table next to the chair, plumped up Viljoen's pillows then beckoned Verity over to the window. 'Come and see the view of our famous blue hills.'

Verity followed and stood beside her to take in the view. A flawless sapphire sky spooled over bleached fields, and the blue hills in the distance, but all she could think about was what she would do next, and how she would be able to communicate with Viljoen.

'He had such a brain,' said Elize, 'it's tragic to see him like this. He gets very frustrated not being able to speak, but he does understand. Sometimes you get a response if he's up to it and feels like obliging. He does one blink for yes, and two blinks for no. I'll leave you to pour your own tea. I've put his in the yellow plastic baby cup there. He can suck on the inbuilt straw, if you don't mind helping him? Okay then, I'll leave you two to catch up,' she said as she patted Viljoen on the shoulder on her way out.

Verity picked up the old-fashioned china teapot and poured herself a cup, spilling some on the tray as the pot trembled in her hand. She sat the teapot back down, picked up the sippy-cup, and held it to Viljoen's thin lips, now as blue and as cracked as the town crater's rim. She watched in fascinated horror as his lips pursed then slackened as he gripped and sucked at the straw.

After a few sips he flopped back exhausted against his pillows.

'I'm sure you know me, even if you only remember my name, so you must realise this isn't really a courtesy call,' Verity began. 'But I'm not here to do you any harm, although I admit that for many years I bore you only ill-will.' She watched for a reaction and saw a faint flicker of eyelash movement. 'I came to see you because I thought you might be able to answer some of my questions, but I see that might not be possible, and that's frustrating for us both. Still, let's give it a try. Elize says it's one blink for yes, two for no. Did you like your tea?'

Two blinks.

'I don't blame you. I wouldn't like an insipid brew in a plastic sippy-cup either. Do you know who I am?'

One blink.

'Good. Are you pleased to see me?'

Two blinks.

'Not surprised, but as I'm your only visitor this afternoon, you're stuck with me. How shall we do this? What if I provide a scenario and you interrupt with two blinks if I get it wrong? Okay? You oversaw National Intelligence when Operation Phezulu was uncovered.'

One blink.

'You discovered Operation Phezulu in May 1990.'

Two blinks.

'I know, it was July. Just testing.'

Viljoen peered at her through a faded iris and blinked once.

'Who led Phezulu?'

He stared blankly at her.

'Sorry, that wasn't a yes-no question. Was Imran Malik the leader?'

Two blinks.

'Someone else in exile at the time?'

Two blinks.

'I thought it was the brainchild of the SACP in exile. This is so maddening. Was Tariq Randeree involved?'

One blink.

'Was Tariq Randeree the brainchild?'

One blink.

'Wow. Was Tariq Randeree behind Phezulu getting mixed up with the armed struggle?'

Two blinks.

'Was it Imran Malik?'

One blink.

'I'm here because I am very keen to know what happened to Tariq Randeree. Do you know what happened to him?'

One blink.

'You do? Oh, my days. Did the security police kill him?'

Two blinks.

'Is he dead?'

Viljoen looked at her, eyes immobile, saliva running down the side of his chin, not blinking.

'Is Tariq Randeree dead?'

Viljoen did not blink.

'Could he be?'

One blink.

'But he could also be still alive?'

One blink.

'So, he was alive at some point after the raid?'

Viljoen hesitated, then one blink. He was getting agitated and making strangled sounds. She dabbed at his chin with the napkin.

'How many years were you certain Tariq was alive for after the raid?' Verity put up five fingers.

Two blinks.

'More than that?'

Two blinks.

'So, less than that?'

One blink.

Verity wanted to scream. This was the closest she had come to confirmation that Tariq had lived, at least for a time after she had left the country. Unable to think of other ways of drawing information from Viljoen, she put his sippy-cup to his lips again, then with shaking hands, wiped his mouth.

'Was he in South Africa after we all thought he was going to Swaziland?'

One blink, a pause, then two blinks.

'He was in South Africa some of the time?'

One blink.

She ran through all the countries she could think of that Tariq might have spent time in, but got nothing but the double blink. Viljoen lay back on his pillows exhausted and stopped responding. Whatever the man knew he would be taking it to his grave. As pathetic as he was, she couldn't find any pity for him in her heart. She'd wished him dead so many times but now felt no urge to smother him with one of his pillows, although as she looked at him then she thought he might have thanked her for it.

'I will leave you in peace,' she said pushing down her mounting frustration, 'although I doubt you live in serenity with what must sit inside your head. I have nothing more to say but this, only you can know who you truly are.' He looked vacant, his frail arm tremulous on the arm of his chair. She fumbled for the words among the remnants of her schoolgirl Afrikaans and repeated, 'wie jy is, kan net jy weet.'

After saying her farewells to Elize, Verity left the farmhouse.

The late afternoon was still warm, but she found herself shivering, the hairs on her arms standing upright. She drove down the dirt farm road at a lick, dust billowing behind her, unsure of where she was headed. She found herself in Tumhole, Parys' black township, driving along unfamiliar streets until the track ended at a fringe of tin shacks backing onto fields of stubbled grain. Smoke rose from piles of garbage beside a vendor roasting mielies on an open grill, while a toddler squashed into a discarded car tyre, regarded her with curious eyes. With her head resting on the steering wheel, she processed the idea of Tariq being alive while she had been holed up in dingy bedsits in London, looking for work and waiting for the ANC to allow her out of the freezer. I was discarded then and I'm an intruder now, here where I have no business, she thought. She turned the car around and headed back to the Riverside Bed and Breakfast.

When Verity arrived back at her room she poured herself a glass of water and wandered down to a secluded part of the garden near the river's edge. She found a bench under some willow trees and sat listening to the movement of water and the rustle of leaves. She ran over in her mind the fact that Tariq was dead, but that he had lived during those crucial years when she was exiled, and the country waited for its new democratic government. She wanted to plunge into the waters of the Vaal River and pit her body against the ferocity of its current, but the river was too wide and the current too strong, even for a good swimmer like herself. Her heart lifted when she saw a cluster of nests hanging like straw baubles from the branches, and she began to slowly calm her emotions. She sat stone still in silence until one or two little black faces peeped out. With growing confidence, the tiny yellow bodies of the Southern Masked Weavers followed, until many more of them began flitting in and out. She sighed with pleasure, feeling grateful for their trust. Sergio would have loved this, Verity thought. Some of their best times had been bird watching, with a backpack, and binoculars their only encumbrance. 'Why did you have to go and leave me, Serge?' she asked, realising she had spoken out loud. Then quietly she said, 'I need to explain to you why I started on this crazy journey in the first place,' and she imagined his reply. *You don't have to explain, cariño. I know all about first loves.*

She realised then that she was exhausted, emotionally, and physically, down to the bone. It was time to call it a day on this futile search, she thought, and there and then decided to check out of the hotel when she got back, and before returning to London have a short break in the Drakensberg. *Good idea cariño,* she imagined Sergio saying. *Go to those mountains you have always missed and mend your fragile heart.*

21

Verity flopped onto her bed when she got back to the Piazza and checked her phone messages. There was a text from Simeon Sikhakhane asking that she phone him back as soon as possible. She was spent and wondered if it could wait until morning, but it sounded urgent.

'Hi Simeon, Verity here,' she said wearily.

'Oh good, Verity, I was beginning to worry you wouldn't get back to me in time. You remember I talked about that former security policeman, Kabo Molefi? He's agreed to meet you, but it has to be tomorrow. I'll give you his number now. Call him to confirm you'll be there.'

'Wait, slow down,' said Verity, 'let me get a pen.'

'Have you had any luck with your other meetings?'

'Mixed,' said Verity as she retrieved a pen from the hotel desk. 'I met Viljoen.'

'Now that name is a blast from the past. What was he like?'

'Well let's just say that deservedly, life has been less kind to him of late. He thinks Tariq is dead, but that he was alive for longer than some may have thought. If he can be believed.'

'Well, I hope Kabo can shed some more light on it for you. You ready then?'

'Fire away.'

Verity scribbled down the phone number on the Plaza headed note pad.

'I don't know where to start thanking you, Simeon. You have been so kind and so helpful. It's been great catching up with someone who is just themselves, and without agendas.'

'I try Verity, and don't be too quick to judge other old comrades. Everyone is doing what they think best to get by. I hope all goes well with Kabo, and if you are staying on for a bit, please do let me know and we can meet up and carry on reminiscing.'

Verity said goodbye to Simeon and sat staring at the number on the pad. Just one more go, she thought, nothing ventured, nothing gained. She punched in the number on her phone and after some time, a man's voice answered.

'Yebo?'

'Is that Kabo Molefi?

'Who's asking?' came the gruff reply.

'It's Verity Vargas, Saunders, Simeon's friend.'

'Oh, okay.' There were muffled words in the background and then, 'sorry, I keep this number only for certain contacts, and you didn't sound like one of them. I'm a man of many cell phones,' his voice now more assured.

'Simeon said you're willing to see me.'

'Uh huh. I might have something for you, but it's not a conversation for over the phone. Can you be at my place in the morning, but like really early, no later than five a.m.'

'I'll be there,' Verity said without hesitation.

'Good. Do you know how to get to Meadowlands?'

'I know it's part of greater Soweto, on the Orlando East side, but beyond that my memory fails me.'

'From where you are, take the R41 then get onto the M70, the Soweto Highway. That takes you more or less straight there. I'll send you a dropped pin with my location in Indoni Street, there's no number but you'll recognise my terracotta wall, it's the only one. I'll see you then.'

The next morning, mystified and still bleary eyed, Verity entered Molefi's dropped pin into her live-drive app. It said the journey would take twenty minutes, although in the past she remembered it felt like Meadowlands was on the other side of the world.

The R41, bracketed by commercial properties plastered in billboards, was punctuated by multiple four-way stops which slowed Verity down. At each one, as she slowed, she glanced at the time and began to worry she would late. The road was busy with trucks and minibuses, more than she would have imagined for the time of day. Street sleepers shuffled out of doorways with cardboard mattresses under their arms, their crusty skins in want of water and care, passing overflowing litterbins and gutters full of fast-food containers flipped along by the wind.

As she joined the faster-moving Soweto Highway, her mood lightened, more confident she would not be late for her scheduled meeting. She took a deep breath and saw through the rear-view mirror the deep crimson sky of the breaking dawn. The road narrowed as it fed into Orlando and as the grid-pattern layout of Meadowlands came into view, Verity gripped the steering wheel in nervous anticipation. The matchbox houses still stood but there were more shops and businesses than she recalled, more cars parked on the streets and more satellite dishes in evidence.

Despite the early hour the former township was waking up, with groups of young office workers heading for the station, and women standing chatting at bus stops. As she slowed to identify street names, a man leaning against a lamp post reading a newspaper, raised his chin in casual greeting.

Indoni Street was more prosperous than others she had driven through, with many of the houses having been extended upwards into double storeys, or outwards over what once would have been the neighbouring plots of smaller houses. Verity pulled up outside one of the latter with a terracotta wall that spanned at least four of the original matchbox plots. A couple of dogs pressed themselves into a strip of shade along the wall, their tongues out, panting against the rising sun. As Verity got out of her car two teenage boys, who were sitting side by side on the pavement, watched her with unblinking eyes.

Kabo Molefi's house was visible through the bars of a large electronic gate, as was a top-of-the-range silver Mercedes sitting on the driveway. A rotating sprinkler spurted out water as it sprayed the lush green lawn in front of the house. Verity looked for an intercom, then saw there was a pedestrian gate set further along the wall. She pressed the buzzer next to the door cam and heard faint chimes from somewhere inside. The door opened and a woman dressed in a royal blue domestic worker's uniform and apron silently ushered Verity into a vast entrance hall beneath a glass-roofed atrium, where she asked her to wait.

From the atrium, and through open bifold doors, Verity looked out to a large garden, with water features, a pool, and the inevitable braai area. Beyond the walls Verity could hear the sounds of Meadowlands waking up; dogs barking, neighbours talking loudly, breakfast pans clanging and parents telling children to hurry up, and then from behind her, the slap of sliders on the marble tiles. They heralded the appearance of Kabo Molefi, dressed in seersucker shorts and a navy T-shirt with Givenchy written across his slightly pigeon chest.

'Welcome to my humble abode,' he said. 'I understand from Simeon you're here after a long time away. Welcome back.'

'Thank you, Mr Molefi, and thanks for making the time to see me.'

'Call me Kabo, for heaven's sake,' he said, sinking into a wicker chair and indicating for her to take the wicker sofa opposite.

'You have a beautiful home,' Verity said.

'That's very kind. I have been fortunate enough to make money in business.' He looked at her from almond brown eyes that sat over high cheekbones and a generous mouth.

'And you decided to live here?' Verity felt herself colouring as she realised how what she had said must have sounded.

'It may seem strange when I could easily afford a house in the northern suburbs, but I'm a Soweto boy at heart. I don't want to live like an umlungu, hiding behind walls and moving in and out with my tinted windows up, and my eyes down. I prefer the vibe in Meadowlands.'

'Did you grow up here?' Verity asked, recovering her composure, and relieved he hadn't taken offence.

'Yes, in this very house. Although of course back then it was just one small part of what stands here now.' He pointed to his right. 'That room through there was my grandparents' house. They were among the first families to be forcibly removed from Sophiatown and dumped here in Meadowlands with their scant possessions. But that generation was resilient, man, and they brought the spirit of Sophiatown with them.' He began to whistle a tune.

'Of course, Meadowlands,' Verity said. 'I remember they used to play it at anti-apartheid rallies.'

'That's right, but it was written by Strike Vilakazi in the fifties at the height of those removals.'

'Well, you've certainly done very well for yourself. Your parents must be very proud.'

'Proud of this,' he said looking around, 'but not proud of everything I've done.'

'You mean when you worked for the security police? Simeon told me about that. It's why he thought you might be able to help me.'

'Eish, I wish that fellow wouldn't go round shooting his mouth off about it. Back then if someone had so much as suspected me I could have ended up necklaced. You know how the townships were. Nowadays the consequences aren't quite so, how shall I put it...consequential.' He snorted. 'But that kind of reputation can affect my business. People still favour those who were on the same side as themselves if you know what I mean.'

'I'm sure Simeon wouldn't talk openly about it to just anyone. We go back a long way, and he wanted to help me.'

'I would like to think so because there's a lot of us in this city with murky bits to our past. But he has helped me out in days gone by so anything I can do to help you, I'm at your service.'

At that moment the woman who had greeted Verity at the gate carried in a tray with a jug of mango juice on it. Verity noticed that there were three glasses.

'Help yourself,' Kabo urged her, 'coffee and rusks are on their way. So, tell me what do you want to know? Simeon said it was something to do with the raid on the ANC safe house in Swaziland back in the eighties.'

'In part. It's mainly about Tariq Randeree. I understand that when Imran Malik was captured you were there and someone else was killed. I know it wasn't Tariq but after that he seemed to completely disappear.'

'Everything you have said is correct. I was at the raid and in fact I was the one who killed the guy.'

'Why, who was he?'

'A Swazi and a very loyal domestic worker, who unfortunately came at me with a knife while I was searching the house. My colleague was outside by the car guarding Malik and we didn't realise anyone else was there. It was a pity but there you go. As for Randeree, he definitely wasn't around.'

'Who commanded the raid?'

'It was a certain Captain Openshaw who oversaw the raid, but he didn't execute it, and he copped it from Major Anton Viljoen afterwards. He was mega pissed at him for not getting Randeree along with Malik.' Molefi paused, poured himself a glass of juice and drank it down in one go. 'It wasn't long after that I decided to leave special branch before word got out and I ended up encircled in flaming rubber.'

'Was there anything else you picked up in the raid? Anything about Tariq at all?'

'Not that I remember, just the usual ANC and SACP propaganda leaflets and then a ton of Soviet literature, which I passed onto Viljoen's team.'

'So why did Simeon say that you might be able to help me if there was nothing else to be learnt from the raid?'

'I know a lot of people, Verity, and what they have done. Some of them owe me big favours. You don't get all of this,' he said waving his arms about him, 'without having your fingers in a number of pies,' he chortled. 'But there are also people who owe you nothing but just stick in your mind. One of them was this junior guy in the branch back then.' Kabo let the silence hang between them. 'He was unusually interested in Tariq's case at the time and may remember more about it than me.'

'You really enjoy this cloak and dagger stuff,' Verity said, trying not to sound too impatient. 'Who is he and what might he know?'

'His name is Karel Prinsloo. I'm not completely sure of what he knows, but he's here and waiting to meet you.'

*   *   *

The early start and pre-dawn drive had put a strain on Verity that she only just acknowledged. Whatever energy she had mustered to get to Kabo Molefi's house on time was evaporating as fast as the dew that had all but disappeared from his lawn.

'Just wait here, he'll be with you shortly,' Kabo Molefi said. 'I have to leave now but make yourself at home and stay for as long as you need.' With that he necked his mango juice, waved away Verity's effort at thanks and left by the front door. She heard the deep throttle of his Mercedes starting up and the whine of the electronic gates as they slid aside for his exit.

Verity went out into the garden and stood under a sky turned yellow and shredded with cloud, her thumbs tucked into the waistband of her jeans. The air was still with barely a ripple disturbing the surface of the pool, but inside she churned with doubt and fear. After a minute or two an outhouse door opened and a man in his early fifties crossed the lawn. As she squeezed her brain, trying to think where she had seen him before, he spoke.

'Hello, Virity,' the man said softly.

She took in the flaxen hair and smooth-shaven baby-face, and then it dawned on her.

'Jan Niemand?' she said squinting into the sun, her temples

throbbing.

'Ja, nee, my real name is Karel Prinsloo.'

'Whatever your name, you're the man who swapped my three-legged bed for a sturdy one!'

'Ja,' he laughed. 'I did, hey.'

His hair was no longer cut with military severity, and he looked more relaxed both in his stance and the way his long fringe now flopped across his forehead.

'Shall we go inside and sit down? Apologies for making you drive to Meadowlands in the small hours, but before we part company I hope you'll understand why it was necessary.'

Verity followed Karel Prinsloo back inside and sat down next to him on the sofa.

'How do you know Kabo?' she asked.

'I don't really know him, although we were in the force together years back. I left that life behind a long time ago, so when he got in touch I was suspicious, but I agreed when he said it was you and that you wanted to know what happened to Tariq. So where to begin, hey?'

'Start at the beginning,' Verity said, 'We have time, it's only just dawn.'

'The beginning is the part I prefer to forget because you see, Virity, I was there when Tariq was tortured. What they did to him was inhumane.' Karel's words stole out in staccato fashion, his eyes fixed on the middle distance. 'There were others too who had to endure Kobus Swart's cruelty, including yourself, but Tariq got the worst of it. After what I witnessed there were times I wondered if I'd ever be able to live with myself. It's surprising, but somehow you do. To keep on existing, you bury things deep and carry on. You still know what happened. You know what you did, or in my case didn't do, but you push the sights and sounds of it right to the back, keeping them buried as deep as you can, hoping they won't resurface.'

'You were there when Tariq was tortured?' Verity asked, reaching for the arm of the wicker sofa as if to steady herself.

'Ja.' He hung his head. 'I wanted to stop it, but I was new in the job and I was scared. I didn't know who would listen if I reported it. So, I just looked on, and did nothing. I tried to make it up to Tariq, but the thing is, Virity, before I say anything else, I need to know I can trust you. You can never speak of what I'm about to tell you to anyone, hey. Some things remain too dangerous to talk about, even today.'

Verity nodded.

'If you did it would provoke revenge from quarters that are still dangerous.' A tight band of apprehension spread across his jaw.

'You can trust me,' she said. 'I mean who am I going to tell anyway. I'm going back to London in a few days.'

'Not a word about it in London either, I'm deadly serious, hey,' he said, folding his arms.

'So am I, Jan Niemand. I'm a loyal old thing and you were kind to me back then.'

'Ok, here goes then,' he said, taking a deep breath. 'After Swart's torture I brought Tariq salves and painkillers, and he was thankful. There was something about the way he held himself, despite the brutality he had faced. There was something almost noble about him. Truly I began to admire the man then. After he was released from prison, I didn't think I would see him again, but then one morning, I was walking along Battery Beach, you know, the last white beach next to the one for Indians and Coloureds. I saw a row of Indian fishermen, and as I like to fish myself I went over to see if they had caught anything. I was standing between their rods and bait buckets when I heard a voice behind me asking me why I wasn't at work. When I turned around it was Tariq.'

'I know the place. Tariq used it as a meeting spot with white comrades. You could stray from one zone to another and have a quick conversation.'

'Ja, that figures and I don't think it was a coincidence he was there then.'

'What did he want?'

'He said that he missed the conversations we had when he was in prison. I was pleased, even flattered. But then he said he needed a small favour, a one off, and he asked me if I could get him the security police file on himself. There was nothing small about that favour, I can tell you.'

'And you agreed?'

'I don't know why but I told him I would see what I could do. I think I didn't want him to see me as being in the same camp as Swart. I had access to all the files and when I read his I thought it would be no big deal. There was nothing in it he didn't know already, nothing that would give me away.'

'So, you met him again then, to hand it over?'

'Ja, at the same place but in the steep part by the dunes. I showed him his file, he read it then asked for files on a couple of other people. He implied that if I didn't then he could let my bosses know I was an ANC sympathiser. What could I do?'

'Yes, Tariq could be ruthless when he wanted something.' Verity said.

'It was nerve-wracking, I can tell you man. It just needed for someone senior to want one of those files and to find it had gone missing for all hell to break loose. Sometimes he'd miss an appointment, other times he'd forget one of the files behind. It got too much for me and I told him I wanted to stop. He kept saying, just one more, then just one more and then there were the veiled threats if I didn't do as he asked. It was through those files that Tariq came to know who the spies were and the askaris. He, and I presume others in the ANC, knew exactly who was under surveillance and what the security police were planning to do with them.'

'Were you a secret sympathiser?'

'Nee man, I never shared his views. In those days all of us in the security police thought all communists were also terrorists. I was very conflicted. To this day I don't know if what I did was right and I know there are people who if they knew about it would kill me.'

'It was brave of you.'

'Not brave at all, Virity, I was scared shitless. Every time there was another car bomb or the discovery of an arms cache, I wondered if my actions were indirectly responsible.'

'So why did you do it then?'

'I couldn't say no to him. It was partly guilt about what happened to him, but I was also a victim of Tariq's charm, a bit like you I suspect. Ag, Virity, I may as well tell you, I was in love with the guy. I think he suspected how I felt and used it to get the information he wanted. I knew he was using me and I worried that he could expose me or that he would reveal my sexuality. I would have lost my job, and my mother would have been devastated.'

'Those were tough times for anyone the state or society classed as different,' said Verity trying to take all this in. 'I remember you talking fondly about your mother when you came to see me. You always seemed to come when I was at a particularly low ebb, almost as if you knew. Did you know?'

'I kept my ear to the ground, but I'm sure sometimes it was just a coincidence.' He offered her a modest smile. 'I came to see you because Tariq asked me to keep an eye on you.'

'So, you were in touch with him after my arrest?'

'Ja, it wasn't long after they first picked you up. He showed up at my house in the middle of the night dressed like some kind of vagrant. I guess he thought that it would be safe for him, because my place wouldn't be under surveillance.'

'After all that trouble I went to trying to get him out of the country,' Verity suddenly fumed. 'And he was alive, and still in the country, so Viljoen was right. But why didn't he get in touch with his family? They were worried sick.'

'Tariq was playing a dangerous game and he didn't want to implicate them if he got caught.'

'But he implicated me, and he implicated you.'

'Ja, that he sure did. He used me, he used you, and he used that young girl, Amira. One time I had to fabricate a raid on the Motala's house because he hadn't had time to return some files to me before he left.'

'Where did he go?' Verity couldn't bring herself to ask directly if, when or where Tariq had died.

'He left for the GDR while you were still in prison, not long after...after what Swart did and...well...he left thinking that he would be safe there and as soon as the negotiations taking place resulted in a political settlement, he would be able to legally return.'

'But that didn't happen?'

'No.'

'What did happen, Karel?' Verity asked, as the knot of unknowing that had always been in her gut, began to untangle.

'The Berlin Wall had just fallen, and that place was in chaos. We still had Tariq under surveillance, so I tracked him through our own intelligence. He and Imran Malik had fallen out over the future of the SACP. Malik wanted a workers' republic like the GDR and Tariq was after a softer kind of socialism like Gorbachev was promoting. It was all a bit beyond me, but we kept detailed tabs on it because it was relevant for understanding the different positions of people who would be involved in the negotiations in South Africa.' Karel shifted his weight from one hip to the other as he formulated his thoughts. 'Something didn't smell quite right, and I did some more digging. What I found concerned me. I believed that Tariq was in danger from Malik.'

'Because they disagreed on the direction the SACP?'

'No, not that.'

Verity waited, the tumult in her mind wrangling with the sounds of a Meadowlands morning now fully awake; the agitation of idling cars, the distant blast of a boombox, the pock, pock of a ball being bounced next door, and the noise of school children bickering.

Karel got up, went outside and stood staring into the swimming pool. Verity followed and stood next to him under a sun now in full furnace.

'What then, Karel?'

'Phezulu,' he said after a beat or two. 'During the negotiations Malik took credit for the whole thing and downplayed the significance of its communications side. He presented the operation as if it was his brainchild, a military plan for armed insurrection, then offered it as the sacrificial lamb to end the armed struggle. As a result, he was hailed as a man of peace. Tariq was furious and threatened to come back and expose him. I think Malik was always threatened by Tariq's brilliance, you could hear it on the tapes we had of their conversations, but in the end it was the lesser man who won, because he had the greater personal ambition.'

'What do you mean?'

'I wanted to warn Tariq, but I didn't know how to reach him without exposing myself. I never thought...but it is possible... no in fact it is highly probable...if our intelligence was to be believed...Imran arranged to have Tariq killed in the GDR.'

'So, he is dead then,' said Verity as she let out a long slow whistle. 'Were you able to confirm it?'

'As close as I could. I heard discussions on the surveillance tapes we had for Malik, conversations about having to get rid of someone. They never used his name. Then our own security sources went cold on Tariq, not another sighting, not another word about him. Later there were reports of a body found in a flat in the GDR, a brown man with no papers, no identification. It must have been Tariq. I felt it, I could hear it in the voices of the other players we had under surveillance. It was enough for me to know, but not enough to be able to bring it all out into the open. I couldn't give his family closure as it would have meant revealing myself and so once again I stood by and said nothing.'

'And Imran got away with everything, another beneficiary of the Bonfire of the Vanities.'

'Ja, nee, I had a good old laugh when they burned all the files. Many of those buggers thought they were home and dry, but I still had a record of every shit-faced traitor in town.' He gave a three-note chuckle. 'I could still expose Imran, Virity, but what would be the point? He's dead. Maybe it's time I had my own little bonfire and put my own files on the braai.'

'Maybe you're right, but thank you for sharing this Karel, at least now I know. I don't blame you for staying quiet and you can trust I won't say a word to anyone. Tariq's mother still thinks he's alive and even if she were to be told the truth, her addled mind would not believe it anyway. But there is one more thing I wanted to ask you...did he know about my miscarriage?'

Karel nodded. 'I was on duty the night it happened, Virity. One of the black warders came running in saying Swart and his drunken gang were causing trouble in the cells. I rushed down and banged on the gate of your courtyard and shouted. They took fright and left. I thought that was that, but the next day word went round after the laundry staff took away your bloody sheets. To this very day Swart doesn't know it was me at the gate, or that I was the one who reported him. As far as I know Tariq never knew what Swart did to you, I spared him that. But he did ask me about you and the pregnancy before he left. It was why he asked me to keep an eye out for you in the first place. He was devastated when I told you'd lost the child. He was really looking forward to being a father.'

'So, Tariq did care,' Verity said softly, then unembarrassed, she leaned across and hugged Karel Prinsloo as tears spilled from her eyes.

22

Under a solid azure sky, the majestic peaks of the central Drakensberg came into view. Verity drove past the communal lands, still presided over by traditional leaders, that hugged the foothills of the mountains and memories of the times she and Tariq had shared there came flooding back. How young and vigorous they had been then.

The thin stream of early afternoon traffic slowed as it peeled into the small town of Winterton, which Verity thought could pass for a small English town if you ignored the dusty pick-up trucks and the barefoot pedestrians. Having booked herself into a cottage for a short break before heading home to London, she pulled up in front of the town's trading store to stock up on supplies. Outside rough-hewn pallets were piled high with sacks of maize meal and five-litre tins of cooking oil. Locked cages, bolted to the wall, held rows of bottled gas and beside them informal vendors sat on upturned crates, watching over their small pyramids of fruit and vegetables.

Inside the store Verity wandered up and down the aisles beneath chugging ceiling fans and flickering strip lights, past shelves that were well stocked but with limited choice. It reminded her of the stores of her childhood when toothpaste was either Pepsodent or Colgate and the only brand of jam was Koo. She stocked up on supplies for her stay, some bread, ham and cheese from a deli counter, then tins of baked beans, Chakalaka, sardines and corned beef. On her way out she purchased some green beans, tomatoes and avocados from the street vendors.

When she arrived at the main farmhouse of the cottage she had rented, the owner, was waiting for her. He looked like a seasoned man of the mountains in his khaki shorts, knee-length socks and well-worn veldskoene. He greeted her heartily, before climbing into his bakkie and leading her up a long single-track road to the cottage. It was a traditional dwelling of the kind built by early British settlers, with a green corrugated-iron roof and a deep wooden veranda running across its width. Below on either side of the steps were beds of pink Azaleas.

'It's beautiful,' Verity exclaimed, getting out of the car.

'Glad you like it,' said the owner as he ushered Verity up the wooden steps, yanking a jumper that had been left on the wooden balustrade. Pulling it on he said, 'the days are still warm, hot even, but the evenings can get quite cold. There's a wood burner in the living room, and extra wood in the shed, now come and see the view.'

The cottage overlooked the farm's dam, as big and picturesque as a natural lake. Reflected in the water were the hills of the Champagne Valley and beyond, the mountains themselves.

'It's glorious.'

'You can swim in there if you are feeling brave enough, but it's freezing this time of year. There are some nice walks on the farm though, so feel free to wander. The dogs may accompany you, especially Enzo our Jack Russell, who thinks he owns the place. I don't think I've forgotten anything,' the man said as he pulled down on the sides of his moustache, 'but don't hesitate to ring the house.' With that he wished her a pleasant stay and left, his bakkie spewing dust in its wake.

Verity took her bags from the car, unpacked her supplies and after making a cup of tea curled up on one of the cracked leather armchairs on the veranda. Finally, and slowly, Verity began to decompress. As she looked out over the water, she realised how much she needed this time alone to process what she had seen and heard, to calm her ricocheting emotions. She wrapped herself in an old merino blanket to keep off the chill of the encroaching night and wished Sergio was with her, curling his arms around her, the feel of his solid frame against her back. She thought about the first night they had shared a bed. He had snored like a steam train, but she had favoured his rumbles and snorts over her long nights alone, when her homesick sobs were the only sound in the room. These she replicated now as she buried her face in the blanket.

'I miss that you loved me even when I was unlovable, even when my breasts slackened and the skin on my arms sagged. At least you'll never have to grow old, you'd have hated that. But I need you, Sergio, I need you with me so I can explain to you why I'm here.'

'It's fine cariño,' she imagined him saying, because Sergio was never a jealous man. *'Go to where you were once happy with your first love. Remember your lost baby son and also remember that I never minded we never had a child of our own. Go walk in your mountains while your heart is still fragile and know one day it will mend.'*

Alone in that quiet valley, where even the barbets and hoopoes were silent in their nests, she stared at the dark silhouette of the mountains, a giant heave of rockface formed millions of years before, and she felt like an insignificant speck in the grand and mysterious universe. The blackened sky was filled with stars and she imagined one of them was Sergio, still burning bright, his eyes lit from the inside. 'You cloaked your darkness in brightness, as you did mine,' she whispered to him through the breeze.

*   *   *

The following morning, as Verity stood on the veranda composing herself before a day of walking in the mountains, a white-and-tan Jack Russell bound up the steps, wagging his tail.

'Hello, you must be Enzo,' she said, reaching down and scratching behind his ear. 'Have you come to invite me for a stroll?'

They walked, Verity and the dog, through a clearing in the woods and out into the open veld. Wreaths of smoke drifted from homestead fires around a cattle kraal across the way. Women were taking washing down from a line, their cackling laughter echoing across the valley as a toddler moved between them on unsteady legs. His mother stood a few paces behind, letting him find his way. He tottered, fell, turned to check she was there, then pushed himself up, bottom first. Verity watched, first laughing, then crying. If her little Owen had lived she would have wished to be like that mother, allowing him to venture forth, sure in the knowledge he was safe and with love at his back.

South Africa was in need of a mother like that, Verity thought, wiping tears from the corners of her eyes. The new nation had been ripped yelling and screaming from a tattered womb, attended by angry midwives like Kobus Swart. She could never forgive him. He had been a bastard then and was unrepentant now. Although she understood that he was the monkey, and not the organ grinder, she would never be able to forget. And the organ grinder himself, Major Anton Viljoen? Even as she had stood before his crumpled form holding his plastic sippy-cup, she had not found herself vengeful but had realised that death is the great leveller from which no one is exempt. In the end Viljoen had got his just deserts, living out his last days diminished and humiliated, and as for Openshaw, he was no more than one of life's mercenaries who had provided himself with a narrative that he could live by.

They walked on, back to the dam, where the oval of black water was fringed by dark earth and the pale fawn and buff of delicate grasses. The temperature was mild after the chill of the night. She striped off and walked into the water, as Enzo lay down on the bank and watched. With a sharp shock and few bold strokes behind her, she gave into the subversive joy of swimming naked. Lying on her back, the warm top layer already touched by the sun held her like a hammock, cloaking the cold depths just inches below. She dabbled the surface with her palms and pushed thoughts of her captors to the depths below and out of her mind, trying to think instead of the good people she had met, people like Simeon who still wanted to make something decent of the country, and Louise and Hanneli who were doing the heavy lifting in building a better country for the future. 'It was worth coming back for that alone,' thought Verity.

When a cool breeze puckered her nipples, Verity flipped over and swam back to the shore, clamouring out onto the kikuyu grass soft under her feet. She lay for a while in the sun to dry off and then made her way back to the cottage with Enzo at her side. Once there the dog did a good line in sitting and begging, so she opened a tin of corned beef in a dish and watched as Enzo devoured it all.

'You are going to have to stay behind now my little friend,' she said. 'I have some more walking to do, and I need to do this hike on my own.' Enzo trotted outside and lay down on the veranda.

Verity prepared a small backpack, made up some sandwiches, slathered herself in factor fifty sunscreen and set off in the car for the start of the Okhahlamba Trail. It was a circular walk of alternating gentle inclines and challenging gradients, and the hike took all her concentration and energy.

As she walked, she thought about Tariq with whom she had last walked in these mountains. She wondered why, after so many years had passed, she had held on to the hope that he was still alive. Had she wanted proof that he had been the cad she had come to believe him to be? In many ways he was, she thought, as she huffed up the steepest parts of the trail. Even at the height of their passion his love for her had been conditional and in the end, Tariq had been as callous and manipulative as Imran, even if he had put his cause above personal ambition. She berated herself for having wasted her anger on those apartheid brutes when she should have been directing it at Tariq Randeree. The bastard had used her, and Karel and Amira, treating them all as expendable, as useful idiots. But he hadn't, as she had supposed for so many years, selfishly headed off to some sunny uplands.

At a place called Blindman's Corner she rested and ate her sandwiches. She pulled out a folded-up piece of paper she had carried with her from London, in the hope, the belief even, that she would find Tariq alive. It was a ghazal by Mirza Ghalib called *The Mistake.*

All your life, O Ghalib,
You kept repeating the same mistake:
Your face was dirty
But you were obsessed with cleaning the mirror.

She smiled, then screwed the paper into a ball and lobbed it over the edge of the escarpment. How many of us, who throw ourselves into struggles and causes, are really trying to fix ourselves, she thought, forgiving Tariq, because after all he became the man he was in the face of an unjust and cruel world, one he felt compelled to try and change for the better.

Sitting with her back against a large rock, cool in a shaded cut, brought to mind the concrete floor of her cell, lying there cold in its chill, unable to move. No matter how hard she tried, she could not shake off the memory and Verity began to weep. She wept for the children of the valley without proper shoes, the drifters in Winterton with no money or jobs, the freedom fighters who never got to see freedom, and the people who would never know the beauty of these majestic mountains. She grieved for her father who died too young, for her mother who tried so hard to understand her mystifying daughter, and for the lost years of affection with her sister. She cried for Sergio and Tariq who both fought for life in their own different ways, and then she cried for herself, fearing she would never again dare to fight and to love with such abandon.

The sun paled and Verity made her way back down the trail, hurrying to reach the lower contour path before it got dark. As she descended past vertiginous cliffs which reared up from grassy inclines, she stopped only to watch a Rock Kestrel hovering overhead, its wings barely moving, as it scanned the landscape for prey. Verity breathed in the crisp dry Drakensburg air, lines of sweat ran from her crown down the back of her neck, and she remembered that she too had been a dreamer who had flown into danger with passion and without fear. No one can unbraid the story of their lives, only reclaiming the strands they want to remember, she thought. It all counted, what she had chosen to do with her life and what others had done with it.

It was late by the time Verity arrived back at the cottage, and the sky was deep and dark. Enzo lay waiting for her on the veranda. and as she sank down into the leather armchair, overcome with fatigue, the dog curled himself across her feet. She dozed, listening to the layers of sound offered up by the night, the rustle of grasses around the dam and the hoot of a night owl. A wind got up, wisps of her hair brushed Verity's cheek and she was woken by a distant rumble of thunder. The sound made Enzo whimper and as she wriggled her toes to alleviate the pins and needles that had set in, he jumped into her lap. Verity began counting the gaps between the thunderclaps. They became shorter as the storm got closer and the lightning flashes became increasingly vivid against the dark backdrop of the mountains.

Enzo whined again and put a paw on her arm, his soulful eyes fixed on her face.

'It's okay old thing,' Verity told him, holding him close. 'It will pass. Everything does.'

ACKNOWLEDGEMENTS

I hope people read the acknowledgements in books because this novel would never have been written or published without the support of many people.

First thanks are due to the team at Epoque Press, for the creative energy they offer and inspire, especially Sean Campbell whose enthusiasm, ideas and suggestions have been invaluable. Thank you Sean for knowing exactly when to yield and when to hold firm.

A thank you hug for the small but perfectly formed 'Covid Cohort' on the MA in Creative Writing and Publishing (MACW) at West Dean College of Arts in Sussex: Sara Bryce Gordon, Emma Matovu, and Mary McKeever. They together with our larger alumni group - Lucy Crewdson, Richard Avery, Jenny Browning, Jim Green, Catherine Sutcliffe, Emma Ward, and Fiona Morgan – taught me what good writing can look like and the importance of dedication to the craft.

My tutors on the MACW at West Dean contributed enormously to the making of this book through their professional expertise and warm approach. I am eternally grateful for what I learned from Domenica de Rosa (aka Elly Griffiths), Mick Jackson, Beth Miller, Bethan Roberts, Lesley Thomson, and Laura Wilkinson, as well as an amazingly talented and inspiring array of writers-in-residence. Special thanks are due to Mark Radcliffe for steering this wonderful MA, and for his unfailing support and belief in my project.

Beyond the beautiful house and gardens of West Dean, others have been kind enough to act as first readers: Paul and Brit Adams, Charlie Beall, Rod Bolt, Shireen Hassim, Kim Segel, and Laura Wilkinson. I am hugely grateful to them all for their time, thought, meticulous reading and ideas.

Meadowlands Dawn would not have seen the light of day without the support of many friends. In Chichester I so appreciated the beds, meals, and general cheerleading from Norma Atkinson, Pam Beall, Kate, Declan and Ursula Carlin, Rebecca Hughes, and Kieron O'Hara. In London and surrounds, Cathy Campbell, Owen Crankshaw, Naila Kabeer, Nazneen Kanji, David Lewis, Caroline Moser, Susan Parnell, Tracey Petersen, Gordon Pirie, Ann Perry and Anthony Swift, Sonja and Harold Roffey, and Susan Valentine were all there with coffee, food, and willing ears. I am also grateful for the interest and indulgence of my wonderful colleagues at LSE Cities and on the SOAS Board.

In Italy where the kernel for this book first germinated and where the final edits were completed, I was nourished in every sense of the word by Suzanna Hopwood and Nicky Road, Nazneen Kanji and David Lewis, Rachel Lewis, Gabrielle Lorenzi, Barbara Lorenzi, Tony McNamara, Elina Roddick, Antonello Rubechi, and especially Marcella Zoe. The warm presence of other friends and neighbours in Montagna made this solitary vice less isolating, and so further thanks to Rita and Cristiano, Aurelio and Marcella, Moreno and Giovanna, Ofelia and Luigi, Maria-Laura and Claudio, Mario and Luisella, Federico and Evalina, Raymondo, Severo and Guiliana, Alessandro, Andrea, Guilia, and Palmiro.

I am indebted to the following people for allowing me to cite their work: Karen Press, for the extract from her poem, Cured; Michael R. Burch for permission to use his translations of the 19th century Persian and Urdu poet, Mirza Beg Asadullah Khan, known as Mirza Ghalib or simply, Ghalib. The other citations of Ghalib's poems were sourced from Scroll.In, PoemHunter.com and the classic poetry section of The World's Poetry Archive (2012).

Last and above all, I am thankful to Charlie, Andie, Lily, and Ted Beall for being a continual blessing and loving family.